How To Throw a Psychic a Surprise Party

a Book of Short Fiction

by

Noreen Lace

REaDLIPS Press

Acquisitions: Della Rey

Editor: Jack Odman

Art Direction: Rebecca Brooke

Cover Photo: Noreen Lace

Cover Models: Citllali Madrigal, Jesus Perez, Priya Singh, Laura Matache, Alfred Tahmasebi.

Background Art: Leydee

Copyright © 2019 ReadLips Press
Los Angeles, Ca.
All rights reserved.
ISBN: 978-1-7331813-2-7

GRATITUDE

Much appreciation to my friend and, in some cases, writing partner, Jo Rousseau. Your presence continues to be a blessing. Your kind words and thoughtfulness guide me in all I do.

Collections have some binding element; this one has grown organically from being rooted in the possible to allowing strings to diminish and the firm grasp on reality to dissipate in order to explore the surreal. There is more empathy in my work these days. Perhaps it's a sign of growing wiser, of allowing life's changes to wash over me, and to strive to understand others.

I struggled for a year or more with "How to Throw a Psychic a Surprise Party" wondering what was missing. I stumbled upon it while meandering the French Quarter of New Orleans and befriending the most unlikely of psychics for a card reading. Although my told fortune may not have been accurate, I understood the story needed more of the best parts of humanity: empathy, growth, and change.

Whereas Paper Wasps and Bowie and the Basket Case remain more grounded, The Healer's Daughter blooms with passion and mysticism while The Crier moves on to question our society's loss of tenderness.

I long for those endless summer days of writing West End, working and reworking sentences for beauty and rhythm instead of having some critiques indicate – Story is King! Story, of course, is important, but so is the package in which it's delivered. Writing without passion and beauty is dime store chatter. In some of this collection, you'll see the beauty of language mixed with the passion of the storytelling. In others, you may notice story at the forefront.

Much love and luck,

Noreen

TABLE OF CONTENTS

Noreen Lace

The Healer's Daughter

Death lifts off Mom like ash in a cool breeze. I'm four and walking behind her; the grass butting the sidewalk at her feet wilts and dies as the low hanging leaves from the trees turn brown when she passes. My mother walks a steady pace, charred gray and black, with pieces gently flaking off and taking flight. She turns, and the front of her, half her face, her arm, and part of her hand appear burned to a crisp, but she's smiling. "Come on along."

Although I skip a step as if to catch up with her, I make no real effort to take the outstretched hand or to stay close behind her.

We cross the park near our home; people pass us and smile, a neighbor walking her dog waves, and another calls hello. No one sees what I see. Many people don't know where we've been. My mom is not always charred, sometimes she's melting sickly olive-green about her shoulders and waist, occasionally molten red on her hands and arms. It all depends on where we've been and what she's done.

A bus ride away from our apartment near the park, we stretch our legs toward a monochrome blue-green house set back from the road. As we approach, a steaming hot orange sears its base and corners. I pause at the door and step back. My mother is in her nice black skirt and red blouse, a jacket hanging over her folded arm, and I'm in a dress and shiny black buckle shoes that Mom makes me wear when I go with her. She smiles and says softly through her teeth, "Honey, this is work." Her blue-gray eyes sliver, so I know I must go.

Someone leads us through a house filled with people whispering and looking on, eating turquoise food, and stacking their bodies in blue corners. We pause in a thick corridor where the walls are dark teal and the stone floor tiles are the same; the homogeneous shades continue with us on the console tables, linens, and to stairwell with a door at the top. The wide hall is dense with dark colors and the scent of decaying wood, and I can barely breathe. Mom tells me to sit in a chair placed against the wall as she disappears behind the door. I stare at the tapestry on the adjacent wall, not wanting to look at the indigo people meandering about me. The tapestry has patterns of triangle designs touching at the tips, separated by thin lines; although the shapes start out yellow, orange, and brown, they turn to hues of teal, blue, and green, with burnt umber lines ready to burst into flames at any moment.

A woman sits on the stairs not very far from me, knee to elbow, hand to chin, her mind a million miles away, or possibly just feet away in that room with my mom, and maybe her mom. A man touches her back with his hand and whispers something into her sapphire ear. He paces away from her to the table at the end of the hall. It's filled with sandwiches, treats, and wine bottles. He pours a glass of wine while azure children tiptoe behind him and sneak sweets from a tray.

I force my eyes to the cerulean stone tiles on the floor and try to sip in little breaths when an ultramarine hand stretches into my view with a fresh tan and white cream puff. I thank him as he steps back and fades into the background. The woman glances over, her face puckered and peach. She offers a weak smile, and turquoise leaks out of her mouth and covers her.

I'm not hungry, but the pastry smells good like sugar and butter, and it feels warm in my hand. I take a bite and the cream spills out the side, onto my hand, dress, floor. Another woman sees, brings me a napkin and smiles sympathetically. The door opens and my mother appears. She is pale and sweaty, her hands and arms bright orange; the color deepens at her ears and blotches around her neck, but her face is her face, her hair is her hair. The blue people converge on her and they make dense round sounds with blue and brown mouths; the man takes a thick hand of folded, blackened bills from his jacket and hands it to her; she takes it, placing it in her blouse. The woman offers her a carved wooden box; she takes that too.

My mother reaches out her hand for me and says something in those round words, but it sounds like it's coming through water and it takes me time to understand. When I try to stand, I feel too thin, like that tapestry hanging on the wall, as if I get up, I'll crumple to a jumbled pile on the floor. When she opens the door and I see the outside, a rush of fresh air and yellow sunlight blow in and I hop off my seat. I don't take her hand but skip out the door and onto the flagstone walkway.

An older woman calls from the back of the driveway; she's not blue or brown or orange, but she's happy, saying words neither I nor my mother understand, but she hands my mother a live chicken and clasps her hands together, offering bows of her head and shoulders. The burnt orange of my mother's hand stains the chicken as she tucks it under her arm. The chicken, clucking and struggling, relaxes and quiets as it stares at me.

I walk behind my mother; the tangerine fire lighting up the back of her neck, dripping off the ends of her hair like raindrops, the box under one arm, the chicken under the other.

We drop the chicken off at our neighbor's house. When we get home, my mother makes me a sandwich of white bread and cheese with green spinach and red tomatoes, but the fire in her hands is dying down, changing to brown and yellow, which leave fingerprints on mushy dough. I push the sandwich away.

She tilts her head, "Not hungry?" She can't see how death lingers on her.

I shake my head.

"Too much cake?" She points a brown finger to the white spots on my pink dress. Her eyebrows lower. Although her eyes are more blue than gray, she's serious all the same.

I am hungry, didn't finish the pastry after it spilled all over me and the good parts were gone, but I don't want to talk to my mother. I just slide my head slowly from side to side.

My mom pulls the sandwich back toward her. "Go change and go out to play, nothing til dinner."

Outside is a safe place, fresh green and clean air with the park right across from our second floor apartment where my mother can watch me. There's always a neighbor or two and other kids, and soon my mother appears on the porch with a glass of iced tea, her book, and the rosary dangling through her fingertips. The rosary works magic on the last of the orange and brown and yellow and, soon, even her neck is no longer marked.

My mother is known as a healer. She doesn't advertise, nor does she search for people to heal. They find her. She tells me that since she was a little girl, she's been able to help people. It used to be with small things, but it grew. She sometimes works a regular job, in an office or at a local shop; healing works by word of mouth and people pay her what they can.

My mother takes what she's given. There is not a discussion of fee. Some people pay my mother in dollars, some in jewelry, sometimes in chickens that she gives to our neighbor, Jacinta, who has her own house. They give her whatever they have, and sometimes they give her more than they can afford because they are grateful for her help.

"This is a gift," she says, "and must be shared." Sometimes, when we are low on food, she sends me to Jacinta for eggs from the chickens or milk from her goat. When we are low on money, my mother smiles softly and pets my hair. "God will provide."

I realize, at some point, that everyone does not experience the world the way I do. The world is bright, vivid colors, and people aren't necessarily white or brown or black, nor are houses beige or yellow or battleship gray, and no one notices the death shrinking my mother as she heals the sickness of others.

She believes someday I will be able to heal people. But when I look at her, pale and sweating, bathed in the hues of someone else's illness, I have no desire to try.

After I start kindergarten, we play a game called *what do our parents do*. I say, my mom helps sick people. The teacher says, "She must be a nurse." I shrug.

"What about your father?"

I stare at her in confusion. She tells me I can sit, but everyone else has an answer for that question.

That day, when my mother waits at the gate to walk me home, I ask, "What does my father do?"

She chuckles and shrugs as she holds my hand, so I try again. "Where is my father?" Because some kids said their fathers lived in different places.

I expect her to say Austin or Up-North, like a few of the kids at school, but she looks at me and then away as if she's remembering something. "As I recall, he said he had something to do. Then he never came back."

I stare at her for a long time, wondering if it was because he saw her colors and didn't like it. "Did he not like you?" I ask.

She holds on to the railing as we climb the stairs to our apartment and belts out a big bellied laugh. "Maaayyybeee." When we get inside, she

7

helps me off with my sweater and says, "He didn't know about you." She pauses and adds, "Even I didn't know about you then. But he gave me the best present ever."

I know she means me, and I accept her answer because that's what I'm taught to do.

Later that school year, a big kid from the second grade comes over to where I sit and play with my friends. "Hearya don' have a daddy. He left cuza you're weird."

I sit and stare at him. There's a thin red line around his mouth and tiny yellow dots around his ears. People have all kinds of dots and stripes and colors in them and all around them. I see them all the time, but don't always know what they mean. Jacinta is lit with bright yellow like a shining sun, and our teacher glows pastel pink. When my mom's not healing, she sparkles with light green shimmers like newborn plants sprouting from the soil. I'm used to these colors. But some people are sick in other ways than physical illness. This I've seen but didn't understand. I stay away from these people and don't say anything to them and, usually, they don't say anything to me.

The next day, when the boy starts again, I stand up and walk away. The third day, he finds me playing tag on the yard with some kids from my class. He yells loudly, "hearya mom is a nurse, but she makes people sick. She's an angel of death."

"No, she's not." I position up to him, too angry to be afraid that he is twice my size.

But he got what he wants, which is a reaction, and he goes harder at me. "Yeah, she's down at the hospital giving them her death touch." His friends and some other kids gather around and giggle and make other noises.

The boy looks paler than before. He has green spots inside of him and yellow around his eyes. I know when the yellow is around the throat and face that people get sick, not terribly sick like dying, but out of school or work for a few weeks with coughing and sneezing.

"Then you better be careful," I say to him. "Because she's not the only one who has the power to kill."

The other kids squeeze in tighter and go silent for a moment.

I point at him. "You're gonna get sick. You're gonna get real sick. And maybe you're gonna die. It all depends on how nice you are to people."

"Oh yeah, sure. Like you can make me sick. Yeah, go on now."

The school bell rings and everyone scatters. That is our signal to line up for class. I don't see that boy the next day, or the day after that. I know the sickness put him in bed for a week or two.

When he does come back, he brings me a present. That red line around his mouth is almost gone. "I'ma sorry. Don't maka me sick anymore."

I push out my chin in victory as I take the blue sparkly wrapped gift. He walks away, and I open it in front of the kids, candy and hair ribbons, which I give to my friends. I don't like to touch or take things from bad people. When I see that kid again, he plays far away from me.

Some of my classmates stay away from me too. At recess, no one wants to play ball or tag, so I sit on the benches and read. Sometimes a teacher tells me to go play, so I walk around the yard and find a shady spot.

One day, my teacher's pink glow is faded, and there's a spiral of red glowing dots around her right side. At the end of the day, Mrs. B calls me up. "You've been staring at me all day inappropriately."

"What is inaprodiate?" I ask.

She smiles warmly. "Have you been staring at me, at my shirt?"

I nod.

"Why?"

"You have red dots on your chest."

She drops her gaze and checks her shirt. "I don't see any red dots."

"They're inside." I point to them.

She smiles again. "You cannot see inside my shirt."

I nod, agreeing with her. I find this is best to do when people don't understand me and want me to understand them.

Sometime later, Mrs. B begins gazing at me in odd ways. In another month, we have a substitute. By the time we have a new teacher, I am an outcast. Even when a new kid comes, I hope for a new friend, but it ends by the lunch bell. Whatever the kids whisper, the new kid must hear. I accept no one wants to talk to me; I keep my head down and don't try anymore. Even the adults treat me differently. When I'm called to the office for whatever reason, they're not as friendly. They glance at each other before approaching the desk; they take my note or paper or words and say thank you, their eyes on me the whole time.

Finally, I ask my mom if I can go to another school.

She chuckles, "Why, honey?"

"There's a bully." I give her what I think is a good reason.

"Did they hit you?"

I rock my body from side to side.

"Life is full of bullies, hon. There's one or two in every school, so changing wouldn't make sense. You've got to stand up to them."

I think for a moment and try the truth. "No one talks to me. No one likes me there."

"No one likes you?" She pulls me into her arms and hugs me. I let her because she hasn't healed anyone lately and her shoulders aren't green, her waist isn't bruised, her arms aren't orange. "How could that be?" She baby-talks, "my sweet, lovely little girl. They must all be madly jealous of your beautiful little soul." I let her cuddle me because I need it and maybe she does too.

"Sometimes," since I'm being honest, "I don't like when you heal. You're funny after." I didn't know how to explain the colors that stick with her sometimes for a few minutes, sometimes for a few hours, and once in a while a few days.

"Funny? Aren't I funny all the time?" She twists her face to make me laugh, and I do, but then I lower my head, not sure what else to say.

"That's Mommy's work, hon. Mommy has to help people. Maybe, someday, you too will help people. Want to try?"

I busy my face in my mom's neck. I breathe in the scent of her clean renewed skin, her apple blossom hair, the mintiness of her breath. My mom is like the spring after she heals from healing others; she blooms. But I never want someone else's sickness on me. I don't want to bring it home, leave it on the furniture, the glasses when I serve tea, or have the shower drain etched with orange or blue or brown as if someone's painted bruise peeled off in streams.

"Jacinta's cat had kittens."

I perk up. "Yeah?"

"And, I was thinking, maybe, if you're a good little girl, help Jacinta take care of them so you learn how..." She tilts her head, her lips ready for the next word.

"Yeah?" I say excitedly to urge her to go on.

"If you can learn how to take care of them real good, I'll let you bring one home on a trial basis."

"Explain this trial." My excitement is tempered by the memory of a television show with a man in a black robe surrounded by a big wooden bench.

"That means if you bring one home, you have to take care of it. You have to feed it and clean up after it. If you do that, then you can keep it." Her face turns serious, but her tone remains soft.

I jump off her lap. "I'm getting a kitty!" I scream. "I will feed it every day." I dance in circles. "And I'll give it a bath every day."

My mom laughs.

"And I'll walk it too. Can we buy a leash?"

Her voice is a sing-song happy laugh. "I don't think you walk a cat."

"Oh, please, please, Mommy."

"Okay, yes." She stands up and heads toward the kitchen. "Now, here," she calls for my attention as I dance in circles with a pretend cat in my arms. "You go on down now to Miss Jacinta's house, take her these biscuits."

I grab the container of biscuits and run for the door. I take the steps carefully; my little legs struggle to move faster and, once I get to the bottom, I run down the street to Miss Jacinta's house, not even turning back to see if my Mother watches from the door like she usually does.

Miss Jacinta is a thin, small woman with long black and gray hair that is tied up in an orderly bun. Although she has a big house and yard, it's messier than anyone else's because of the chickens, the cats, dog, and the goat that she tries to keep tied up out back. I rush through the screen door; it slams behind me to announce my arrival. Eggs sit on the counter, they are probably for me to take home. I slide the container of biscuits next to them.

"Out here, honey."

I follow her voice to the side door and a screened-in porch. The cats are in wooden crates; the mommy in one, the kittens in another, both snuggled in old towels.

"Mami esta sick." She points to the big gray cat. "Won't feed bebes." She holds up one of the kittens whose eyes are not yet open and pushes the tiny baby bottle toward the kitten's mouth.

"Like this, bueno?"

"Yes." She hands me the little kitten and the bottle.

I feed one, then wipe its mouth and pick up another. I watch the mommy cat lay still, occasionally breathing out a soft mew. I know she's dying.

When I've fed and cleaned all the kittens, I pet the mother cat. She tries to purr, but it's low and bumpy. There's a purple bulge in her tummy, close to her back legs, so I pet her gently. Her purr grows stronger, and she meows. I pick her up, lay her in my lap, and try to give her a bottle, but she doesn't want it. I pet her, and the lump shifts.

My hands run up and down her body as I stroke the velvety fur; it's only when I pause I notice the plum stain on my hands. My heart pounds. I pull back and my blue skirt is tinged with brown, my folded legs dyed apricot. Tiny breaths stick in my throat. I don't want the colors. "No. No." I push the big gray tabby back in the box. "I'm sorry, Mommy cat." I jump up and rush through the house. My legs are stiff and heavy; I can't run fast enough.

"Ninita?" Jacinta calls after me. "Que... Huevos..."

Tears streak my face before I'm out of Jacinta's yard. I whisk, crying down the street, stopping for deep breaths only when I reach our apartment building, then another burst of energy pushes me up the stairway. My mother's hanging up the phone; I imagine Jacinta called her. She surveys me but doesn't ask the questions forming on her face. I glance down at my hands, dress, wonder if she sees the fading purple bruising, the discoloration on my dress, the tinge of yellow-orange circling my knees. But, when she says, "What is it, honey?" I know she doesn't.

"Mommy cat is dying." I wail. She hugs me, but I don't hug her back. "Mommy, go fix her. Go heal her."

The corners of her mouth dip. "I can't, hon."

"Yes." I yank her hand. "You fix everyone else, even people we don't know."

"Honey, you don't understand. I've tried; I can't heal animals."

I race to my bedroom and throw myself on the bed. My insides tighten, my stomach cramps. I push my face into the pillow and sob. It's not the mother cat's impending death, but my own fear is why I cry myself sick. The colors frighten me. The scents and sounds and the flakes that come off my mother scares me, and I don't want any of it.

By the time I've wept myself out, I turn my head to look at my hands; only a slight shade of lilac remains. I roll over and inspect my dress, knees. The colors are gone, and I am all me again. I tramp to the bathroom, shaking slightly. I wash the tears from my face; the rest of the color from my fingers swirl down the drain, and I stand there having a silent conversation with the little girl in the mirror. I didn't want this. I don't want the colors on me. I don't want people looking at me strangely. I think of the kids at school who won't be my friends.

My mom doesn't tell people unless they ask for help. Many of our neighbors don't know. Jacinta knows. I think of that mommy cat and all the kittens who need her. I wonder if, as my mom says, I must help if I can.

"You okay, little sweetie?" Mom taps on the door.

I open it and look her up and down. She glows as she smiles at me. "Better?"

I nod.

"Lemonade?"

I follow her to the kitchen and climb up on the chair to watch her.

"Why do you help people?" I ask.

"It's important to help people." She slides the ice filled glass of lemonade across the counter to me and reaches for the special box of cookies. I'm not allowed to take them whenever I want; I must ask, but I always like when she offers them to me first.

"What kind of world would this be if we didn't help people who needed it."

I nibble the ends of the cookie, thinking. "So why do some people not like us because of your helping?"

She gazes down at the table, tilts her head, then looks up at me with a small smile. "Well, hon, some people aren't open to those who are different, and sometimes people are afraid of things they don't understand."

"If I don't understand something, I ask."

"And that's what you should do." She watches me finish the cookie and offers me another, which I refuse.

"Can I save that for after dinner?"

I like the way my mom smiles. Sometimes it's little like a secret, and other times her eyes light up, her lips part, and her face brightens. When she does that, I know she's happy.

"Jacinta likes us."

"Jacinta's a good person."

I slurp down the lemonade and wipe my mouth with my arm, which my mom doesn't really like, but I do it funny so she laughs. Then I take a napkin and wipe my mouth and arm.

"Can I go back and see if Miss Jacinta needs more help?" I don't tell her that I might be able to help the mother cat.

"Of course, honey."

I walk slowly, fear infusing in every step. By the time I knock on Miss Jacinta's door, I'm too shaky to open it myself.

"You okay, Ninita?" Her skinny arm pushes open the screen door.

"Do you need more help?"

"Si, bebes need to be fed every hour."

I walk through the house and wonder if the mommy cat will feel I betrayed her, but she merely mews when I sit down next to the box. I scoot closer and pet her, pet the lump. I've seen my mom do easy things like a cut or a blister on people. I pause as the violet tinges my palms, but the cat purrs and meows, lifts her head and tries to lick my hand, so I keep going. Her body pulsates, that lump moves, she yowls softly. The violet turns to magenta and bleeds through the crevices of my fingers; I use both hands, she makes noises, splays her tummy open to me, I pet more and the lump moves, it moves more; she lays back on her side and yowls and I take my hands away quickly, frightened by the howl.

Jacinta comes back in, "Que? Mami cry?"

There was a purplish, black lump laying near the cat. She stretches and stands up, steps out of her crate and pushes her head against me for a pet, which I give her. She inspects her kittens in the other crate, licking and mewing to them. Their chorus of hungry cries ring out.

"Oh my." Jacinta picks up the unmoving lump with a nearby cloth. "Muerto."

"What is it?" I help the mommy cat who begins to pick up her babies, one by one, by the scruff of their necks and move them back to her crate.

"Sometimes, Ninita, a bebe gets stuck and doesn't come out." She gazes from her palm to me. "It's a good thing it finally came out, Mami would have died." She smiles at the mommy cat. "She's ready to feed her bebes!" Tears sparkle in Miss Jacinta's eyes. She wraps the little thing up and walks away. When she returns her hands are empty and freshly washed, and she put her hands on my shoulders. "I guess I won't need so much help."

"I'll still help though," I offer for fear of losing my kitten.

"Sure, Ninita. Anytime you want, you come help. But you can't take the bebe for five or six weeks."

I wipe the fading plum color from my hands onto my dress as I stand up.

"You don't forget the huevos for your Mami, this time."

The mother cat purrs as she feeds her kittens. At this moment, I don't care about the colors, I helped the kittens, the mother cat, and Jacinta too. My body fills with warmth, and I feel shiny and bright.

When I walk in and hand the bowl of eggs to my mother, she waits for me to say something.
"I think I want to be a vegenarian."

Her eyes round in confusion.

"Cuz I like taking care of animals."

She laughs. "Veterinarian?" And pulls me into her arms, colors and all.

I feel happier than I think I ever have. I no longer bother about the bully or the kids at school. Next time my mom fills with colors or shrinks from ash, I won't be afraid. I'll hold her hand and hug her.

Mirror people

Marnie once didn't leave the house for a half a year before any of us noticed. She was better now, so we thought. She'd refused some invitations, but we didn't notice how many. Jewels came to town specifically to celebrate the baby's first birthday with the family. Marnie insisted, "yes, yes, I'll be there!" But with the last-minute phone call to cancel, it became time to confront her.

When Jewels arrived at Marnie's tiny home in a small, rural suburb, she swore she'd heard conversation inside. There were no other cars, save for Marnie's hunk of rusted junk, and now her own Prius rental; it might have been neighbors, if they cared to hike the distance between houses.

Jewels knocked; curving her ear to the door, she'd heard a snippet or two before all went quiet.

Just as Jewels opened her mouth to call out, the door sucked inward with a whoosh that seemed to reveal it'd not been opened in some time. How long had it been, she wondered, since Marnie had left the house this time?

Marnie held the door to her shoulder as she stuck her head between the opening. "Jewels!"

Jewels, arms crossed, waited for the door to open. "Are you going to let me in?"

"I'm in the middle..." Marnie glanced over her shoulder.

"Do you have company?" Jewels craned her neck in attempt to see over Marnie's head.

"Not exactly. Uhm." Marnie bit her lip. "Could you give me an hour?"

"An hour? No. I drove all the way out here. It's cold, now let me in."

Marnie hesitated. She held tight to the back of the door and stood up straighter. "Yes, yes, of course. How rude of me." She glanced behind the door one more time which concerned Jewels. Was Marnie in trouble? Was someone there? And her language: "How rude of me"? Who says that? "Give me maybe five minutes, ten minutes, would you mind? While I clean my mess? I'm wholeheartedly embarrassed by the state of things in here."

Jewels, arms loosened, nodded. Marnie'd always been odd. We sisters mentioned it often to one another. She was the black sheep, the odd girl out, always needing a little extra care or attention.

Even as a child, we'd witness her stare off at nothing, keep quiet when all of us rambled, hang back when the rest of us rushed forward.

We number nine now, with the birth of the baby. Jewels moved away to college before the youngest two were born. The rest of us meandered about in the same city, visiting each other, visiting our mother, and helping with our younger siblings. With the exception of Marnie, all of us decided pretty young what to do with our lives, college, marriage, career.

She'd jumped from job to job and often collected disability when they allowed her for her panic disorder. Some time had passed since her six month disappearance and we weren't well aware of her activities of late. We were all pretty certain her anxiety hadn't presented any further problems, but none of us could pinpoint the last time we'd seen her either.

Jewels walked back to her car where she grabbed a sweater and walked back toward the house; her foot barely tapped the top step when the door swung open with ease and Marnie welcomed her. Jewels embraced her momentarily, then glanced around the room searching for evidence of her company or habits.

"I thought I heard you talking in here." Jewels swept herself to the couch, where she dropped her purse.

"No." A slight shake of her head. "Probably the television."

The television was an old box model. The screen brownish gray, the buttons dirty silver, color worn off the dials. "Do they still make those?"

Marnie ha'd. "No, but I do have a repair guy who can fix it." She touched her hand to Jewels elbow. "Come on in here, I put some tea on."

Jewels followed, struck by these new behaviors. "Tea?" So unlike Marnie to appreciate proper, if not outdated, social etiquette.

But once the tea was on the table, Jewels overcame her suspicion and rededicated herself to the purpose of her visit. Marnie, seeming to sense the onset of questioning, jumped up from the table and returned with a silver serving tray heaping with cookies. "They're homemade."

Jewels lifted one to her mouth and nibbled to be polite. Although full from dinner, she took part in the ritual. The cookies smacked of fresh lemon, soft, yet lightly crisped on the corners. "You made these?"

Marnie laughed. "Yes, who knew I could bake?"

Jewels set the cookie on the rim of her tea plate and noticed the design of the cup, glanced at the silver serving tray, then at dark stained oak table which Marnie could never afford. "Where did you get this?" Jewels ran her hand over the polished wood.

"Trash." She sipped her tea. "It's amazing the things people throw away!" The excitement on her face implied honesty.

"So, you have been getting out."

"Oh, yes, regularly."

"Who helped you?" Jewels wondered if there was a man in Marnie's life, maybe in the house now, kept him a secret for some reason. That explained the sounds of conversation, the motivation to improve her cooking skills, even the possible lack of appearances at family events.

"I did it." When met with Jewels' disbelief, she added, "I came back and got a screwdriver, got the legs first, then see..." she pointed to the center seam, "I unscrewed it piece by piece. There's even another section for the center to make the table larger."

Jewels nodded.

"The family's angry, huh?" Marnie leaned in. "I owe everyone an apology. I lost track of time." She spoke emphatically, "Then, the car wouldn't start."

Jewels believed most of it, but something was off. Then again, she thought, something was usually off where Marnie was concerned. Jewels opened her mouth to respond when Marnie again leaned forward. "How long are you in town for?"

More oddness. Previously Marnie sat back and accepted the reproach, unpracticed in the art of deflection. "A few days."

Usually Marnie offered her a room, even near begged. "Stay out here, everyone is so far away from me, I never get to see you." And Jewels prepared to accept; she'd even carried the overnight bag in her car. When Marnie didn't ask or offer, Jewels said, "I thought I might stay here."

With that, Marnie popped from her seat. She gazed at Jewels, half smiled. "More tea?" She didn't wait for an answer before she rushed off toward the kitchen. Jewels glanced around the elegantly decorated dining room. She might believe Marnie retrieved these things from the curb, but the style didn't reflect her younger sister; someone helped her.

When Marnie didn't return right away, Jewels went in search of her, through the kitchen and followed the sound of whispering where she found her sister closing the door of the closet.

"What are you doing?" She jumped nervously.

"Looking for you. What are you doing?"

Marnie waved her hand and ha'd again. "Just putting things away. The house, you know, was such a mess when you arrived."

This Marnie was unlike the Marnie we all knew.

Moving quickly away from the closet, she again touched Jewels' elbow and said, "how about that tea?"

Jewels lagged, pulled open the door of the closet: Brooms, linens at the top, sweaters on hooks, covered pictures or frames in the back. She followed Marnie back to the kitchen. "You're always asking me to stay."

"And you're always refusing," Marnie shot back. "So there's no reason for me to have assumed that you might stay this time."

"True, but..." Jewels found this new Marnie vexing. People change, of course, they do and should; However, Marnie remained stagnant in habit and personality, so to change over this single year puzzled us.

Jewels attempted another tone, the more accommodating approach used with other sisters. "I'd hoped to visit with you since it's been so long." Jewels walked up behind her little sister, touched her longer hair. She put her hand on her shoulder, the way she would when they were teenagers. "I've missed you and want to make certain you're okay."

Marnie smiled. "Of course." There was the girl we all knew and loved.

When Jewels returned from the car, bag slung over her shoulder, she pushed open the door and found Marnie with her head in the closet, so engrossed she didn't noticed Jewels behind her. "Is this where I should...".

Marnie jumped and slammed the door. "Don't do that. Don't ever do that!" The angry expression caused Jewels to stare at our sister in deep concern. Marnie's shoulders slumped and her posture caved. "Can't you see how you frightened me?" Once again, she placed her hand on Jewels' elbow and swept her other hand toward the hall. "Let me show you your room, I was just moving some things around to make you more comfortable."

Jewels knew she was being handled.

"I just have to move one more thing out of here." She opened the door to the guest room. "We can put your bag here." She motioned to a small table which stood in front of the closet door. "The closet is packed with junk and the door is stuck anyway." The four curved marks in the carpet near the adjacent wall suggested the table had sat there for some time and was moved recently.

Marnie picked up a large rectangular object covered with a clean white sheet. "I'll move this out of your way."

Jewels stopped her, pulled the cloth away. It was an old gilded framed looking-glass. "Gorgeous, you can leave it."

"Not this old junk." Marnie picked it up with effort. "It's uncleaned, old, can't see yourself clearly..." she rambled.

"Let me help." Jewels started to put her hands on the mirror.

"No." Her tone strong, then immediately softened, "No, thank you. You're the guest. Please, make yourself comfortable."

Jewels watched her sister struggle across the hall into her own bedroom. Jewels swore she'd heard mumbling, then her sister clearly said, "It's just for tonight." Jewels strode with purpose into her sister's room and glanced around. Marnie closed her closet door and met Jewels with a smile.

"What is it?"

"I swear I heard you talking to someone."

Marnie ha'd again. Unlike her, really. "I was chattering to myself. People do that when they live alone." She led her sister from the room. "Let's catch up."

They sat comfortably chatting in the living room before their eyes fought to stay open and their voices faded from fatigue. They yawned and called it a night. Jewels was pleasantly surprised; although Marnie hadn't found a regular job, she cleaned houses for elderly neighbors and their friends. She earned enough to pay the rent and have a little extra. Marnie hadn't yet risen to her family's hopes, but she was making her own way, which was admirable, and Jewels relayed Marnie seemed happy.

As Marnie made her way flipping off lights, Jewels picked up her sweater to hang in the closet. When she opened the door, she froze. Beyond the brooms, the closet floor was packed nearly full from wall to wall and on the shelves with the linens, all types and sizes of mirrors. Some faced each other, others covered, still others sat back to back. Marnie returned to the room and saw Jewels in the closet; she rushed to her. "What are you doing?"

Jewels laughed. "I was going to hang my sweater. What are you doing with all these mirrors?"

Marnie shifted her sister and closed the door. "I found 'em." She started down the hall for the guest room, but Jewels didn't move. She reached for the closet, swung the door wide.

"How many mirrors does a person need?"

"I told you." Marnie rushed back and tried to shut the door again, but Jewels held tight. "I found 'em. People throw them away."

Jewels stood still, desirous of a more complete explanation.

"It's bad luck," Marnie pled. "It's bad luck to throw looking-glasses away, did you know that?"

Jewels had never heard such a thing. Of course, we'd grown up with mirrors, a cheval glass in one room, a vanity in the bathroom. Some of us had fancier ones, some preferred plainer ones. But none us had kept them in closets or covered. They were merely a means to an end. Make certain our clothing was okay, our faces weren't hideous, our hair in place.

"It is. So is breaking a reflector, but not for the reasons most people think. Did you know there's a way to get rid of bad luck? If you break a mirror, you must wash all the pieces in a river. See water is reflective and so it washes away the..."

This is what Marnie does when she's nervous, when she's hiding something, or feels we're judging her, she rambles. She caught herself and stopped.

"Washes what?" Jewels loosened her grip on the closet door.

Marnie pursed her lips as she closed the door slowly. "Curses," she whispered. "Washes away the curse." They stood there, Marnie avoiding Jewels eyes and Jewels' rising concern for Marnie's mental health. She wondered if it was a hoarding disorder or if it was the girl's anxiety.

"I just see them along the road. People throw them away. They're really pretty, and sometimes they're old, but it seems like such a waste."

Jewels nodded, glancing around the room. There were no mirrors hanging, none in the living room where they'd spent the last few hours chatting, not in the dining room, nor in the guest bedroom. At one time, a pretty pier glass hung across from Marnie's bed. "Why not hang them?"

"I will. I couldn't decide which one should go where." Speaking slow and controlled, careful now of what information came out in front of her already suspicious sister. "You're not supposed to hang more than one in a room."

"Why not?"

Marnie flipped her hand, half smiled. "You know," she half ha'd. "Superstition. Like a portal or something."

"Portal?" Jewels was unfamiliar with this folklore, which wasn't surprising; none of us really knew much about superstition or urban

myths. We weren't brought up that way. Of
course, we learned things from kids at school,
don't walk under a ladder and throw salt over
your shoulder if you spill it, but we weren't very
privy to other legends.

"Yeah, I forget, really, what it's all about."

Jewels didn't believe her. She strode with
purpose to Marnie's bedroom; Marnie on her heels
murmuring the whole time. "Something to drink?
Where are you going? Is there something you
need?"

"You have no mirrors up anywhere," Jewels
said when she arrived in her bedroom and
confirmed the one across from Marnie's bed had
been removed.

"No, there's one in the bathroom," she
defended.

"What happened to the rest?" Jewels pointed
to the faded outline.

"It's not good to have a mirror across from
your bed," Marnie boasted confidently, then
clasped her hands when Jewels met her gaze.

"Why not?"

"Feng Shui," Marnie chuckled, which turned
into a laugh. "I don't even know what they say.
Like it'll ruin your sexual energy. But maybe I
should put it back because there hasn't been any
sexual energy in here in ages."

Jewels breathed audibly. Marnie yawned,
stretched. "Let's hit the hay," she said in a familiar
inflection that reminded Jewels of herself; the

familiar way she spoke to us. "I understand you're concerned. But all is well. We're both tired. Let's come back to this in the morning."

Jewels nodded. They were tired. Maybe she was overreacting. So her sister collected crap from trash. There were worse things.

They'd said good night at the bedroom doors, much like we all did when we were younger. But Jewels laid awake, pondering their childhood. There might be another reason for the mirrors, but it didn't make sense. Marnie'd never mentioned it again, so we thought she'd forgotten all about it. All of us had; however, that night, laying in the darkness of Marnie's mirrorless guest room, it all came rushing back.

We intended to take turns. None of us believed anything would happen. If we remember correctly, Jewels tried first. She folded her arms as if she held a baby, then repeated Blue Baby, Blue Baby, Blue Baby, and stared into the hand-glass. In the silence, under a blanket in the faux- darkened space, nothing happened. With much enthusiasm, Marnie begged to go next. She enveloped her arms, pushed her face into the reflection, and repeated, Blue Baby, Blue Baby, Blue Baby. In a moment, she screamed, grabbed her arm, and threw the blanket aside, escaping into another room.

By the time we'd caught up with her, a tiny scratch bled on her arm, which the ritual had foretold. After the scratch, according to the folklore, the baby's mother with razor sharp nails would tear at the person who kept the child. The small scrape on her arm was the size of a papercut and we all giggled it off, believing she'd injured herself while running through the house. It was so small, it didn't even need a band-aid.

We'd all forgotten about it until that very night.

Jewels laid motionless, tried to force sleep until faint noises disturbed her. She tiptoed to the closet, moved her bag, set the table aside, and started to open the door when she heard Marnie in the hall.

Creeping out of the bedroom, she saw a small light illuminating Marnie's back as she leaned in to the open closet door. Jewels approached slowly, attempting to discern what Marnie whispered into the darkness. She became certain of more than one voice. As she entered the room, a sound like a man clearing his throat and a movement near the light caused her to spin. A large mirror sat on the couch.

When she turned back, Marnie had closed the closet door and stared at her as if Jewels, not Marnie, had been caught in some strange ritual. "What in the world are you doing?" Jewels asked.

Marnie folded her hands. "You can very well see I was moving that."

"And the whispering?" Jewels crossed her arms and tapped her foot in true older sister fashion.

Marnie ha'd, "I told you..."

"Marnie, I'm very concerned about your mental state." Jewels' anger sparked.

Marnie offered no defense or explanation, but merely glanced at the mirror that sat across the room.

For a second, Jewels thought she'd seen movement from the corner of her eye, but it was just she and Marnie's reflection. "I'm leaving, Marnie. Let the rest of the family deal with whatever is happening with you now. If you're going to lie to me, I'm done."

It'd been Jewels who came when Marnie didn't leave her house for six months. We hadn't even noticed until the holidays came and went and Marnie hadn't that we'd became concerned. Jewels took a semester off college, coaxed her into medical care, drove her to appointments, talked her into trying the medication, and stayed until Marnie began living her life again. Maybe that was latent guilt from the childhood misdeed, but we'd all attributed it to sisterly devotion. We would all want to say that we'd have done it, but the truth was that Jewels stepped up and we let her.

Jewels stalked back to the guest room, tossed her bag carelessly on the bed, and changed her clothes. The sound of whispering emanated through the walls. When she swung around, bag in hand, the murmuring seemed to flow on a cold breeze from the closet. Jewels stepped closer, pulled the door open, the sounds stopped, and again, she was certain it'd been Marnie in the other room. But, on the floor, in the back, a large item covered in canvas; Jewels yanked on the cover. It was so old and worn, it didn't even cast a reflection; the surface more hollow gray than reflective. Jewels slammed out of the room.

Marnie waited in the hall. Quiet voices filled the living room and Jewels thought she'd turned on the television. Marnie swiveled from the room to Jewels and the voices grew silent. When Jewels entered the room, mirrors leaned on the couch, the chairs, against the walls; the room surrounded them in looking-glass. Jewels was convinced Marnie had lost her mind.

"If you'll just stay, I can explain everything." Marnie removed the bag gently from her sister's shoulder, setting it on the floor; she took hold of Jewels' elbow and led her to the center of the room, speaking softly. "Some people believe souls can become trapped in mirrors. Others believe they can talk to spirits through the looking-glass, and some even think their health and future can be foretold by reflective surfaces."

While a few of the mirrors were modern, black framed, most boasted older, wooden, and even ornate, and gilt frames. From the center of the room, Jewels and Marnie were reflected at all angles

"Some time ago, I found a mirror in the trash. I brought it home and put it in the guest room. Occasionally, I'd hear the odd sound, but thought nothing of it. Around that time, I worked for one woman who kept a large mirror near her bed at night, said it was her husband. I just thought she was old and lonely. When she died, she willed me two pier-glasses. That one," she pointed, "I hung on the wall; the other I stored in the guest room. At night, I'd hear things in that room, odd breezes, the occasional noise; it was weird. The clamors at night became unbearable. Every time I went in there, it became quiet, but whether I left the door open or closed, I'd hear voices whispering. I thought I was losing my mind. I stormed in here one night and screamed. Marnie kept hold of Jewels' arm and pointed to the mirror on the adjacent chair. "That's when Mr. McLanahan said, 'my wife is upset that you've not kept us together.'"

Jewels sucked in a breath and shook her head; her sister needed professional help.

"Please, listen before you judge. This is Mr. McLanahan, and that is Mrs. McLanahan. When they're not in here, I keep them in the closet face to face. There is Mortimor Joseph Bailor. He is the one I found in the trash and put in that room. He likes to be alone, and he was causing the problem tonight."

Jewels huffed out the held breath, glared at Marnie. Marnie was either playing a trick on her and paying her back for all those years ago or her sister had lost her mind. Jewels spun toward her bag; she needed to leave, to regroup and figure out how to help her sister.

"Wait, wait. You see that table in there. When I got it home, it was a wreck, stained and faded. I refinished it. Mr. Kepper, here," she pointed, "taught me how to refinish furniture. And those cookies? Could I ever bake before? Janie, there," motioning to the corner, "taught me. I can bake almost anything now."

Jewels pulled away from Marnie.

"Ladies, gentlemen, please!" Marnie pleaded.

At first there was a long silence, but then, "How else do you think she learned to bake?" A voice clearly stated.

"I want to correct any misconception you may have," Mrs. McLanahan said, "I wanted her to keep us together. I did not throw a fit."

Jewels swung around to Marnie's smiling face, her hand held out toward the mirrors. Jewels glanced from glass to glass and at first just saw herself and her sister, but then something moved, someone stirred, faces appeared. Mr. Bailor fingered his goatee, Janie fluffed her hair and smiled, Mrs. McLanahan seemed to relax and glanced over at her husband who smiled at his wife. Other faint images, small movements, strangers, old and young; some seemed to hang back, others stared back at them.

"I'd rather like to go back to my room now," Mr. Bailor gruffed. "At least, in there, I have a purpose."

"Yes, Mr. Bailor, I'll put you back."

"Oh, his job, his purpose. You're just anti-social," Janie said. The younger woman faintly appeared and faded again.

Jewels started to step back and seemed to lose her footing, near fainting. Marnie caught her. "You okay?"

The closet door in the guest room slammed against the wall. Marnie gaped down the hall. "Is that table still against the door?" The bedroom door slammed shut.

"Oh, gosh. He's out!" Janie disappeared.

"Who unleashed that dark mirror?" Mr. Bailor growled.

"Did you uncover the one in the closet?"

Jewels half nodded, still trying to catch up with this new reality. "I heard...."

"I told you to leave me there. I told you not to take me out of that room!" Mr. Bailor came through loud and clear.

"Oh, dear, what will we do?" Mrs. McLanahan said.

"It's okay, dear. We've handled this before," her husband answered.

A cacophony of other voices arose.

"What's happening?" Jewels felt, for the first time in a very long time, out of her depth.

"That's a dark mirror. I didn't know such a thing existed. But then I started feeling ill all the time. Things were randomly falling off the walls.

Everyone started arguing. They're the ones who figured it out."

Jewels shook her head. "Why would you keep it? Throw it away, put it back where you found it!"

"It's not that simple."

"Take me back there. Take me there, now," Mr. Bailor demanded.

"I'll help you," another offered.

"You guys can't do it alone," another voice spoke up.

"Help me." She tapped Jewels' shoulder and headed for Mr. Bailor; together they picked him up and carried him to the room. They forced the door open and set Mr. Bailor adjacent to the swinging closet door. They retrieved Mr. Kepper and Mr. Mclanahan, angling them on either side of the first.

"What now?" Jewels asked.

"Break the damn thing," Mr. Bailor ordered.

"No. She'll be cursed. We'll all be cursed," Mr. McLanahan said.

"Besides you can't just break a mirror," Mr. Kepper offered. "There's a ritual."

"What's the ritual?" Jewels asked.

Marnie walked her out of the room.

"Don't do it," Mrs. McLanahan's and Janie's voices sung out from the other room.

Jewels came back to the bedroom alone, reached deep into the closet, retrieved the dark glass, and set it against the table. The others warned her, begged her, "Get Marnie," one implored. "Cover it!" demanded another.

"Let's see what this is all about." The gray and brown unpolished metal seemed harmless, as if it didn't have a reflection at all, but that was the very problem. Legend dictated, if a person gazed into the reflectionless obsidian, they'd be sucked into a lightless world, a nonportal, where they'd wander a dark world without end, taunted by the embittered souls trapped before them.

"Don't look into it. Don't go near it." They called out. Jewels caressed the frame, eyes locked above the draw of the lackluster center. A cool breeze swept out of it, a barely discernable mist reached out for her wrist and, just as it was about to grasp her arm and yank her in, Marnie appeared from behind and smashed it with a hammer. Jewels pushed the frame to the floor as Marnie continued to smash at it with the metal hammer.

The other mirrors gasped and guffawed, while the dark one howled and growled.

Jewels and Marnie worked quickly to collect the pieces and place them all in the canvas cover, vacuumed and dumped even the tiny slivers of wood and glass into the wrap. Even tiny bits of any broken glass can injure, but dark slivers cause pain for years to come, infections, illness, death. They folded and bound the canvas so the pieces could not work their way out. They rushed to Jewels' rental car and drove like mad to the nearest river. The mirror in the back seat vibrated and hummed, attempting to free itself.

It was nearly four a.m. when they reached the parking area. They dragged the heavy canvas through the dirt and tall grass; it seemed to struggle and lurch from side to side, the girls pitched off balance nearly losing their footing. Once near the water, they waded into the center of the river, holding on to one another. As they struggled to untie the rope and loosen the canvas, they were knocked side to side. They held onto one another lest one be swept away by the rising tide, the pitching canvas, or caught by the streams of screaming mist escaping the river. They shook the last of the canvas, washed all the pieces away, and when the water calmed around them, they knew they were safe.

Arm in arm, they made their way to the shore; soaking wet, they trudged through the dirt and grass to the car, and arrived at Marnie's tiny little house in the suburbs, to a room full of inquiring voices, "what happened, what happened?" As Marnie made tea, Jewels brought the others, even Mr. Bailor, to the living room.

Covered in blankets, they sipped tea on the living room floor and relayed their success to the mirror people.

Jewels filled us in before she'd left town. We all sat silent and speechless, waiting for the punchline. But it never came. We believe Marnie lost her mind and dragged Jewels down with her.

We intend, at some point, to do something to help our sisters, but with the baby so small and our lives so busy, none of us are certain when it might happen.

The Crier

When my sister's husband of five years died suddenly of a heart attack, I told her it was perfectly acceptable to hire a crier. Sarah resisted, moped for weeks, and began disengaging from her life. We had a family intervention of sorts, just our mother, Betsy, sister in law, JoAnna, and me. We caught her one Saturday when she should have been at Gymco, but instead she sat out in the yard staring at the tulips, of all things.

We asked her to come in and sit in the living room, like a civilized human being, made her a cup of zanatea and gathered around.

"Honey," our mother began. "It's been nearly two months, there is no shame in a professional."

Sarah gazed down at her feet.

"I had a good one right after my baby left for college," JoAnna added.

Sarah nodded and glanced around the room.

"Do you need help cleaning out his things? Why aren't you drinking your tea?" I moved closer and put the cup in her hand.

She took the tiniest sip and returned it to the table. "Josh, I'm not ready to get rid of his things."

My mother sighed audibly. I motioned my hand in her direction. Sarah was not usually given to dramatics, but we couldn't let Betsy's baser instincts rule this meeting.

"I just think..." Sarah hesitated, "maybe there should be a period of mourning, of sadness, like maybe I should cry myself."

JoAnna and Betsy gasped, both pushed forward in their seats. It was certainly out of the norm, but as a Health Coach at Gymco I hear all sorts of crazy ideas. Instead of the gym, people want to run outside – as if their senses could manage the environment. I usually give them a supplement and put them on our MockCity Trainer for thirty minutes; the noise of traffic, the lack of temperature control, and the uneven terrain forces the realization of their momentary lapse of reason.

All people need are supplements and a Gymco to be happy. But some people want to experiment. According to the news, a few people who stopped supplementing with zanatea or coffenex ended up in psych wards. Humans lost emotional coping skills years ago. It takes someone special with years of training to inhabit an emotional life.

I leaned closer to my little sister and took her hand. It's an odd thing to do, but as a Health Coach I am trained to talk people down from irrational decisions. "I can list at least a hundred reasons why you don't want to do that."

"Why would you even want to try?" JoAnna slumped back, completely confused.

"JoAnna's got a point," Betsy added. "Nothing good comes from allowing ourselves uncontrolled emotions. I remember those days." Mom was ready to launch into one of her caveman stories, "we had to walk ten miles in the snow uphill" myths about how hard life used to be. No one believed her stories, but they were entertaining.

"Sarah," I said. "What you're sensing right now, all these thoughts of mourning are just the tip of a very large, very deep iceberg. An iceberg, that if you hit, you'll sink like the Titanic and you may not make it back."

Sarah looked up at me, withdrew her hand gently, and nodded. "But isn't hiring someone to cry for you like cheating?"

"No!" JoAnna sprang to life again. She was the expert on this. I'd personally never needed to use one, but she'd had her fair share. People used to hire them for small things, kids moving away or divorce, but these days it was mostly just family deaths and funerals. Criers were expensive, and some people questioned whether they were actually beneficial.

"So helpful. I couldn't even imagine getting all messy myself. You should see what happens to their faces. And, when they wear make-up, oh, no, Sarah, I wouldn't want anyone I know going through that."

Mildly helpful.

"Hon, I hired two back to back when your father passed. Let me tell you what a relief it was to actually get it all out without feeling all those horrible things. You two laugh at me, but I remember when we had to cry on our own; it was wretched, uncontrollable, led some to do horrible things to themselves and to others."

Sarah pursed her lips; she didn't believe her. "It's true," I added. "As a trainer at Gymco, I've read the reports. People used to do crazy things, throw fits, spend months in bed, take pills, and even commit suicide."

"That's an urban legend!" Sarah shot back.

I wagged my head slowly from side to side. Her hands were clasped tightly in her lap. I suspected she'd avoided taking her supplements. She was edgy, and that was the first sign.

"It's not." Betsy intervened. "It used to happen all the time. The minute, the very minute they'd invented coffenex, suicides dropped by half."

I wasn't certain Betsy was helping, but Sarah did give her a long, lingering gaze that I took as if she were getting through.

"It is true, sis. They don't make things like that up. People who do not supplement on a regular basis sink to levels unknown, and they don't end up in good places." I spoke gently.

"Sarah, when your husband dies, it's not the time to lose your head. Think about it. If you want to scale back or something, do it some other time under expert supervision." Betsy's urgency and JoAnna's dramatics played well against my sincerity. I'd chosen the right people for this.

Sarah inhaled deeply and relaxed into her chair. I handed her tea once again; this time she sipped and held the cup close to her lips. After a minute she asked, "How do these criers work?"

"I highly recommend the one I had last time. You will find Banu indispensable." JoAnna flipped through her phone, clicked a few buttons. "I sent you her info. If you don't like her, I have another. You don't want a man, do you?"

I mouthed "no" to JoAnna. No one needs a male-crier. I can't believe they even exist.

"No. I'll try Beanu, Benu, whoever you recommend." Sarah took another sip, and then another. "Geez, I'm feeling much better just talking about it."

We all visibly relaxed. Mission accomplished.

"Maybe after a couple of sessions, we can help you clean out..."

"A couple?!" Sarah looked at each of us. "Do I need more than one? I only want one."

"One will be fine," JoAnna picked up her own cup of zanatea. "If they're good, one session will be more than enough. You'll feel like a new person."

Sarah scheduled the session for the following week. Being naturally apprehensive of the open display of emotion, she asked me to sit in. Having no desire to actually witness the display myself, I planned to sit in another room where I'd be close but not intrude on their privacy.

Banu was a tall, thin woman. Her skin seemed pink and fresh, as if she'd had too much sun. Her clothes fit loosely with long sleeves and pants; I wondered if she was hiding how long since she'd been to a Gymco. But it was probably all due to the regular release of emotions.

"Not a problem, happens often. It's good to have family close during this time." Her manner was practiced soothing.

"How does this work, exactly?" Sarah's voice wavered.

"Well, you sit and tell me what happened, who your husband was, what he meant to you, and I cry at the appropriate times."

Interested, I asked, "Do you find it overwhelming to cry often?"

She smiled thoughtfully as we sat in the living room. "I am trained. But I don't just do crying. I've been hired to worry, to be nervous, and to laugh uncontrollably. Of course, that's my favorite."

"Laugh?" I wasn't quite certain I believed her. On what sort of occasion would anyone find it appropriate or even desirable to laugh uncontrollably?

"Of course! Professional emotional release comes in all forms, expressing a wide variety of feelings. There are even times during a cry session that I might giggle because sometimes memories, and pain, can be bittersweet."

I averted my eyes and smirked. This whole convection of emotions is why people are trained to do this job.

"Did you have your extra cup of zanatea?" Banu asked Sarah.

She did, but I hadn't. All this talk of emotion created a need for more coffenex. I poured myself a cup as soon as I left the room and made myself comfortable in the dining room where I opted for a side view of their faces.

Sarah spoke softly; I could only hear a few things every now and then, but the crier began tearing immediately. At one point, she sobbed openly, which made me draw back in my own seat. Sarah watched with interest, occasionally leaning in. At one point, they even took each other's hands. And, at least once, she did what she said with that little laugh between tears and sobs as Sarah talked about a vacation mix up which had left them stuck in Finland during winter with nothing more than shorts and bathing suits. They'd spent the night with Mai Tais in a hot tub while Jamacian drums thrummed through the phone.

After nearly two hours, they were winding down. I felt exhausted; I stared at the bottom of my cup and wondered if another was a good idea. Sarah excused herself to freshen up, and I stood as the crier made her way to the dining room.

"She should sleep this afternoon. Give her some driftea to help her rest more comfortably." Banu's face was red and puffy; her eyes clear blue, with thin red lines passing through the whites. She hadn't worn make up, but the tears still lined her skin. She dabbed gently with a tissue, and the very act made me want to take the tissue and dab for her. I felt unnaturally drawn to her and desired very strongly to put my arm around her shoulder as I walked her to the door. Although I was at a loss for words, I felt the need to say something.

"This is a valued amenity."

She smiled, "Thank you."

"No, thank you. I see how your services might be effective." It had some sort of effect on me.

"I work at Gymco. I have someone who might be interested." I stumbled over my words. I knew no one who would need such a service, but it's always good to make contacts and be ready in case I'm ever asked.

She handed me two cards. "My husband is a Professional Mourner too. Some men prefer male criers."

I smiled tightly. She'd sensed I was reaching and put me in my place as gently as possible. "Thank you. I'll be sure to mention that."

As she walked to the car, I lingered, watching, before finally closing the door. What might that house be like with all that emotion flying around? I leaned against the frame, considering it.

Sarah reappeared with her face freshly powdered, and her eyes bright. "JoAnna was right. A good crier was just what I needed."

Noreen Lace

Paper Wasps

There's something majestic about the way a paper wasp builds a nest for her offspring. The precise whisp of the wings, the gentle landing, the purposeful movement around the tiny mud colored hanging umbrella, prepping for the day she will become a mother. Wasps haven't graced the eaves of their home in years. Rachel stares through the kitchen window, the clear stream of water running in the sink, until the gentle moment exploded, rocking the windows and shaking the doors.

Beyond the unaffected wasp, across the street in the Water and Power's Lot, a thick column of black smoke rose followed by flames as one of the transformers reacted with violence to the energy drain which a week of one hundred degree Valley temperatures brought on.

Rachel's kids appear in the doorway. As her daughter, Adeara, braces herself in the frame, fearing a second shake, her young son asks, "Was that an earthquake?" and her husband bellows "What the hell?" when the television blacks out.

"Looks like a transformer," Rachel pushes the spicket down, dries her hand on the already damp dishcloth laying on the corner of the sink and brushes the strands of hair from her face.

Her kids rush to the kitchen window and edge Rachel out, struggling for a view. She moves to the front door, watches through the window.

"Cool." Robbie stands on his tippy toes vying for space and a view; at nine, he is four years younger than his sister and a full two feet shorter.

"Oh, calm down." Adeara joins her mother. She snaps a picture with her phone. "I need to tweet this." Even though Adeara's thirteenth birthday passed a month ago, she competes with her mother's height. From the back, they are near mirror images; hair puffed by the heat, black t-shirts, jean shorts.

Neighbors gather immediately, strolling down the street toward the smoke and flames, cell phones in hand.

"Power's out." Kyle runs his hand through his unbrushed hair, stepping in front of his wife to pull open the door. It's Sunday; a t-shirt and shorts after rolling out of bed at noon is his idea of a perfect day of rest.

"Cool, can I go?" Robbie races in front of him heading toward the neighbors chatting at the corner as they film the fire.

"Oh, yeah, go film it!" Kyle offers a tap of encouragement.

"No." Rachel grasps Robbie's shoulder. "Another transformer could blow or that fire could spread."

"You worry too much," her husband pokes.

The fire sparks and blanches, shooting thick black whorls into the air. A wire crashes down in the lot housing the transformers. The group standing at the corner shares a community gasp and some retreat and wander up the street as the fire trucks arrive and obscure the view.

"Can you believe this?" Jay, from down the street, pauses in front of their driveway. "From the looks of it, no power for days."

"Do we know what happened?" Kyle joins him.

Sully and Janet, from the opposite end of the block, raise their wine glasses, "should we bring down the bottle while it's still chilled?"

"We'll need something stronger than that!" Kyle chuckles.

"Got that too." Sully laughs.

Claire from across the street starts for them, hesitates, then continues, her face awash in usual concern. Since they'd become neighbors years ago, every time the thin, young woman crosses the street, the scene repeats; her face furrows, hands fidget, and the hesitant pause, as if she didn't want to bother them, then the slow stride toward them.

"The kids are at their cousins." The pale Claire balls her hands into fists, gently bounces them into one another. One knuckle cracks, then another. "What am I going to do when they get home?"

"It'll be fine," Rachel offers. "They'll have the power back on soon. Do you have candles, flashlights?"

Claire's neck muscles tighten as her head bobbles. "No. Nothing like that."

"I'm sure we have extras."

Kyle shoots her a look over his shoulder, which Rachel ignores. She turns toward the house, noticing the little wasp tapping purposefully on the planter, daintily bobbing toward her nest, building her home under the eaves of Rachel's home. Her forced smile dissolves into a real one. Mothers make do.

The sprite and graying Sully and Janet reappear with a bottle of Johnnie Walker. "Got glasses?" He holds the bottle high like a trophy.

"Honey, get some cups!"

Rachel opens the door, watching the wasp.

Janet passes Claire with barely an acknowledgement, "let me help," and breezes past her. "Open these windows or you'll be suffering tonight."

"Should I open my windows?" Adeara's phone beeps and she disappears toward her room without waiting for an answer.

Robbie rushes in and shoves his phone in front of Rachel's face. "Kevin can see the fire from the other side!" then runs off again.

Rachel reaches for the plastic cups, hands them to Janet.

"Oh, yes. Good idea. Of course, I hate to use these. You know, the environment and all." Janet heads toward the little party on the driveway.

Rachel makes her way from room to room, opening windows, hoping for a breeze. When she rejoins the gathering outside, the impromptu party has closed in on their patio. Claire stands stiff next to the steps, no drink in hand. An electrical company truck has arrived near the lot; the workers attempt to disperse the small crowd. When their neighbor, Russ, calls out, "Could be a week." He smiles like the cat that caught the mocking bird, and asks "You all got generators, right?"

Kyle openly sneers, dropping himself in the only remaining seat. "A week? We can't handle 110 degrees for another week."

Sully chuckles, "I'll stay with my parents before I deal with that."

Touching her husband's arm, Janet rolls her eyes playfully. "You can go to your parents, I'll be at the Four Seasons."

"He's guessing," Rachel watches Russ waddle down the street. "Did anyone see him talk to the guy in the electrical truck? There's a hospital on this grid. We won't be out long."

"Hospitals have generators, backup power." Sully crosses one leg over the other, makes himself comfortable in her chair.

Claire bites both lips. "Oh, dear. A week?"

"Shit! Shit!" Kyle jumps up. "Everyone back"

At varying speeds and levels of concern, the neighbors stand, turn, look. At first, everyone glances to the last whispers of smoke rising in a thin, curled line toward the sky.

"Wasps!" Kyle traces the flight of the single wasp. "Those things'll kill ya."

"They will not." Rachel moves closer to see her wasp. She knows it's a Paper Wasp. Nearly harmless unless provoked. Her office specializes in safe removal of bee colonies and she identifies all types of flying insects by their descriptions. People call with all sort of folklore and fears, and many can't tell the difference between a honey bee and a bumble bee, let alone a wasp from a yellow jacket.

"I've seen them attack a man before. They gather their buddies and sting and sting until your dead." Kyle's eyes light with black label whiskey excitement.

Rachel teases. "Did you see that in a movie?"

"I don't think they're that dangerous," Jay offers.

"Oh, hellya, they are. We had a whole mess of them that first year we moved in." Kyle energizes with story. "We had an expert come out and check them out."

Rachel knows they'd seen few, but hadn't called an expert. The painters merely knocked down the nests and painted over the homing scent, so the wasps hadn't returned.

Adeara shows her face at the door, curious about the commotion.

"Of course, he wanted to charge me a fortune, so I took care of it myself." His voice rounds with bravado. "I got one of those beekeepers nets and put on like three pairs of clothes, and I still got stung. Didn't I, honey?" Without waiting for a response, "Every year since then, I walk the perimeter to make sure they're not building nests."

Rachel smirks. "I remember it differently. Besides, these are paper wasps. You don't bother them, they won't bother you."

"Paper wasps!" he mocks. "As if there is any such thing. Where do you get this stuff, soap operas?" He slides a small smile her way.

Sully works his way down the steps, Janet next to him. "I think he's got you there, Rachel. Never heard of paper wasps. They're called yellow jackets."

Jay adds, "Yellow jackets are pretty aggressive creatures."

Rachel smiles. "Okay, kids, in the house before the wasps get us." She waves the kids inside, an excuse to leave the party and retrieve the nearly forgotten candles for Claire.

"What?" Robbie lifts his face from his phone and swivels his head back and forth.

"For reals?" Adeara follows her in.

"Google it." Rachel searches for candles and flashlights, but by the time she returns Paul's truck has appeared in the adjacent driveway. Their four young kids, all under eight, climb out over him as Claire lifts one by one to the ground.

Rachel waves, candles in hand. Claire calls, "We're good, but thank you!"

Although she's willing to help, Rachel also thinks a mother should prepare for everything and not count on others. Like that wasp, bits of dirt, bits of web, and a little nest hangs strong.

Having said goodbye to Jay, Sully, and Janet, Kyle follows her back in the house, "Hon, you were rude."

"How so?"

"They were our guests and you kept making excuses to come into the house."

"I was preparing for a night without power."

"Okay, Miss-they'll-get-it-back-on-in-no-time." Kyle peels off his shorts, drops them behind the closed front door, and snaps the band of his boxers.

"What are you doing?"

"For reals, dad? Creepy." Adeara heads to her room.

"Hey, I'm not going to sweat to death in this house tonight," he says louder than necessary.

"Can I strip down to my boxers too, Mom?" Robbie starts to unbutton his shorts.

"I prefer you don't."

"What are we going to do all night?" Kyle makes his way to sit his near naked, sticky self on the couch.

"I guess I'll be cleaning." Rachel collects Kyle's puddle of clothes.

"Just leave it. Power's not on, can't do anything anyway."

"Yes, that's a good answer." She says wryly, laying his clothes on the laundry basket before grabbing a book and her reading light to return to the now quiet patio. Kyle stretches his body over the couch, hands folded behind his head, feet hanging over; Rachel pauses, thankful that almost everything she needs runs on batteries.

Remembering the wasp, she angles her chair to watch, but the wasp is nowhere to be seen. Her work finished, the evening approaching, she'd tucked her barely discernable body in the single little hive.

When the kids come in search of dinner, she allows them cereal on the condition they eat an apple too. They sit at the dining table, in the shadow of the setting sun as Kyle yawns loudly, waking from his nap. The house sunk into near dark except for battery operated candles flickering at key points: the kitchen sink, the bathroom, and in the kids' rooms.

"What's for dinner?" He calls as if in a cavern. He finds them sitting at the table, bowls pushed aside and the kids on their phones, Rachel angling her booklight closer to the page. The temperature cooled, but still no breeze; the sweat beads from all of them.

"Tonight is going to be unbearable. What'd we do for dinner? Cereal?" His tone thins and curls.

"There's turkey and cheese." She offers, not lifting her eyes from her book.

"But that's for my lunch tomorrow."

"Use half now, half tomorrow."

"But then I'll be hungry tonight and tomorrow."

"Cheese to go with your whine?" Adeara slips from the table, eyes unbudged from her phone. Rachel smirks into her book.

"Oh my gosh, this phone is almost dead!" Adeara says dramatically.

"Cheese to go with that whine?" Robbie snickers as he, too, slides from his seat. "Mine, too. What are we going to do when they're dead?"

Rachel smiles warmly, widens her eyes, "We might have to talk to one another!"

"Yeah, that'll happen!" Adeara's voice circles back even as she leaves the room.

"Seriously," Kyle idles behind Rachel, "what are we going to do? This is like emergency situation stuff."

Rachel watches Robbie shuffle away. "We'll charge them in the car, but not tonight." They'd have to disengage the electric locks and manually raise the garage door, pull the car out and start it. It's been too hot and too long a day for that.

"How am I going to get to sleep with no games to relax me?" Robbie leans in the doorway.

"How am I going to wash my face in the dark?" Adeara's quiet voice comes from the shadowed hall behind him.

"It doesn't take light to know where your face is, and you can play solitaire."

"What's that?"

"Google..." Rachel smiles to herself. "I'll show you."

When she gets up to search for playing cards, the smell of gas fumes waft through the kitchen. The mud room door stands open. Rachel paces through the kitchen and halts in the garage entryway. She waves until the car window whirs down.

"Are you trying to kill us all?"

He stares at her.

"If you don't want to pull the car out, at least open the garage door."

The car stops idling, Kyle's gaze rests, humorless, on her.

Rachel walks back through the house. The car door slams, the mudroom door slams, and the kids bicker in the bathroom over firstees in the shower. She walks straight through the house to the front patio for a breather.

On any other night, satiated from dinner, Kyle'd relax in front of the television, Robbie would play games on his phone, and Adeara might chat with her newest best friend. Rachel, left alone, could wash dishes, fold laundry, or even continue to enjoy her book. Quietly. Tonight, however, she feels as if she's babysitting someone else's family.

Any other evening, neighbors might sit on their lawn chairs, wave from a patio, or even say hello as they walked their dog; But the temperature outside was only a degree or two cooler than the house and nothing moves outside, even the sun seems stuck in the western sky.

Rachel inhales a few deep breaths. An occasional flashlight or candle show through the neighbors' windows and all is quiet except a low rolling hum. She turns to her own patio, but mother wasp has not awoken. She gazes toward the Water and Power's lot; the smoke nearly dissipated, the truck gone, and their whole grid, save for hospitals she imagines, off. But the low vexing drone continues. Another deep breath and she braves the house to calm everyone down.

Robbie stares blankly at the internetless laptop. "I thought I could talk to my friends on this, since wifi doesn't need to be plugged in."

She places her hands on his shoulders and kisses the back of his head. "Well, honey, the wifi works from a main box, which is over near the television, and that does need to be plugged in."

"I knew that." Robbie frowns in defeat.

"You know what doesn't need power? Cookies."

Robbie half smiles.

By bedtime, her phone boasts the only remaining power. She sets the alarm and, in the morning, she wakes the others, wakes them in five minutes, and another five minutes later. Without the flicker of lights, the hum of fans, the chill of the morning air conditioner kicking on, let alone the loss of music for Adeara, youtube cartoons for Robbie, and a hot shower – yes, even in the summer, - for Kyle, no one moves very quickly.

At her office across town, the phones work, their lights flicker once in a while, but on brown out conditions, the air conditioner stilled. Fans whir and, with the well placed trees in front of the building, they remain comfortable. Only three of the staff of five show and no one calls, so they listen to the radio: Emergency services, hospitals, and fire stations regained power first. The DJ reports that firemen, neighbors, and volunteers checked on elderly people, bringing back-up batteries to those who may be on oxygen. Some lucky residents' power popped to life in the middle of the night, lights ablaze, televisions blasting; however, half the Valley remains powerless.

Since the open office is useless without business, Rachel leaves early to shop for supplies: ice, lunch meat, cheese, etc. She arrives home, lunch in hand, to find her husband, slouching in a chair, Adeara sprawling on the couch, and Robbie on the floor, playing on their phones with fast food wrappers around them.

"No school today?"

Kyle shrugs. "No one went today."

"No work for you?"

"Like they expect me to come in? People are looting all over the city!" he exclaims. "Had to stay here, protect the homefront. Right, kids?"

"Uh-huh."

"Whatever."

Although the radio reports indicated opportunists sneaking into a Toys R Us and a Hobby Shoppe, she hadn't heard reports of homes being burgled.

"What are these?" Rachel leans over to inspect the black boxes attached to their cell phones.

"Solar chargers!" Kyle smiles proudly, pushes himself up to show her. "Runs on solar. Pretty cool, right?"

"Did you need three?"

"Three phones, three chargers." He drops his body back into the chair.

"It's so hot!" Adeara whines without moving. "I can't stand it. Can we go to the mall or something?"

"Yeah, we should go downtown. They have power!" Kyle agrees.

The kids start to stir as Rachel offers, "Everyone had that idea, traffic's been terrible all day. Besides, malls are on brownout conditions. You might drive for an hour or two only to get some place that doesn't have power."

A group groan floats to the ceiling.

"What's for dinner?" Her son rolls over and gazes at her.

"Sandwiches."

"Oh, man. Boring."

"Not sandwiches," Adeara stares at her phone. "Helina's dad bought a generator. Can we go get a generator?"

"Great idea. Home Depot in the Valley is out. We can drive downtown and get one!"

The kids sit up excitedly.

"Maybe call first," Rachel says.

"UGH!" An annoyed group moan chases Rachel from the room.

"Did you call your parents?" She unpacks the groceries as Kyle lifts his gaze toward the wall separating them.

"Why would I?"

"See if they're okay?"

"They're fine."

"Did you check?"

He stands up, clicks a button on his phone, and starts for the back door. "Hi, Mom...."

"Either of you see Espi?"

"Who?"

"The older woman down the street." No response. "Who has the big garden?" Still no response. "Who gives you guys oranges and avocados whenever she sees you?"

"Nope." Adeara's only half listening.

"I'm going to take a walk down the street."

"I saw," Robbie calls out. "When we went for McDonalds. The man in the big Jeep came."

Espi's son, Rachel thinks.

"Good. Was McDonalds open?"

"Not any of the close ones. We kept driving."

Rachel stands at the kitchen window, wondering if there's anyone else she should check on. Her own parents live up north and called her as she drove to work this morning, "You're always welcome here," her mother ended with. She didn't consider it; the power wouldn't be out much longer.

The wasp floats by and up to her nest. She rests for a moment before flying off for another little piece of something. When they'd moved in years ago, the two or three tiny wasps' umbrellas weren't the first things they'd noticed. When the house was painted, the wasps moved on. Spiders moved in, bees visited, birds graced their trees.

Most escaped notice, given the everydayness of life. Her job had taught her the differences between the species and a new respect for their place in the eco-system. One little mother wouldn't present a problem. When her babies hatched and flew away, they could unscent the spot.

Her kids find her motionless at the sink, "So where's the sandwiches?"

"I thought you guys ate."

"Gosh, Mom. That was hours ago." Adeara's tone spikes annoyance in her mother. Rachel reaches for a glass and pours herself tea from a once-chilled pitcher.

"You have tea and you didn't tell us? And Ice?"

There's ice?" Her son rushes to the refrigerator with her daughter close behind.

"The ice is to keep the food from spoiling."

"We can use a little, right?"

Kyle appears in the doorway. "There's ice? Where's dinner?"

"The ice is to keep the refrigerator cold, to keep the food fresh. And, I told you I would make sandwiches." She grabs a napkin, swipes the sweat from her forehead.

"You know, Rachel, you're not making this black-out any easier." Kyle stares her down. "A little ice is not going to kill anyone. We can always get more."

Her usual patience tips on empty; Rachel takes her tea to the shade near the corner of the house, far enough away from the patio so she doesn't hear her family inside. She takes a deep breath and immediately notices a low, near moan of a hum and not the sibilating of a single wasp nor a hive of wasps. She glances up and down the street; no kids play in the heat, no parents call from the patios, no drone from radios, or the hiss of television, just the birds, and that singular wasp building her nest. The neighborhood is Twilight-zone still, a showcase of houses, windows open, doors agape, families inside avoiding movement. Yet that low murmur of buzz continues. Maybe it's always there, in the background, and she hadn't noticed because of the sound-clutter around them.

She glances back at the wasp who pauses to watch her. Rachel half-smiles. *Don't worry, lady, I'm just standing here.* They observe each other for another moment before the wasp continues her work.

The chatter inside her own house rises, becomes closer, louder. The low rumble of "where's Mom? Mom? Mom?" and the door bursts open with suddenness.

"What are you doing out here?" Adeara asks.

"I need to charge my cell phone," her son interrupts.

"I need to charge mine first."

"What about your solar chargers?" She moves toward the kids.

"Honey!" her husband meets her at the door. "Those solar chargers are junk. They're dead already!"

"Did you charge them?"

"What do you mean?"

"Like did you put them in the sun and charge them."

"Yes."

"No."

"What do you mean?"

All their voices vibrate as one.

Rachel holds up her hands to signal for them to stop, or maybe for herself to not lose the last bit of patience in that once very deep well. "Come on. The chargers need to sit in a window or outside – they need the sun to charge."

"Yes."

"No."

"Yes, we did."

"What do you mean?" Adeara finally breaks through the mingled voices. "We're supposed to sit in the sun and use them?"

Her family seems needier than ever. The wasp stops moving; she sits on the nest, observing the family's buzzing.

"They were supposed to be charged when we got them!" Kyle adds.

"Solar chargers – in a box – how much sun did they get in the box?"

"You don't need to talk to me like that!" Kyle raises his voice. "They said charged, so I took the company at their word."

Exhausted and overwhelmed, Rachel blows out a slow breath. "Did anyone, maybe, listen to the news? See when this power outage will be over?"

They glance at each other without responding.

"Does anyone have any power left?"

Consciously or unconsciously and in succession, their hands wrap tighter to their phones.

Just then, Janet and Sully appear and Kyle waves as they turn up the driveway. Rachel offers an embarrassed smile, wondering if they witnessed the squabble.

"Have you heard? Another day or two," Sully says. "It's cooler outside than in our house, so we decided to take a walk."

Janet's weak smile fades as she whispers to Rachel, "yeah, a walk will cool us down," with the intonation of sarcasm. "Heat's getting to us," she adds.

Claire's door opens, and she starts toward them while her husband waits on the porch, their children pour out of the house and sit on the painted wood stairs. She pauses briefly at the end of the driveway to lightly pound her fists. "Do you guys have any ice we can borrow?" She isn't joking. "We went to every store in town."

Kyle speaks first, "No. No one has ice." He glances conspiratorially to Rachel.

"We have a little," Sully strides down the street.

Janet leans into Rachel, whispers again. "Can you believe it? Now he's giving our ice away."

Claire drops her arms, stiff at her sides. "Paul's leaving again tomorrow. Work. I just don't know what I'll do if the power's not back on."

Rachel turns away, tired of hearing the whining drone. The wasp stands still on the edge of its nest watching the growing group of people; Rachel wonders if the wasp is reconsidering her location, too much noise to raise young ones here.

Sully returns with a bowl of ice, passes it to Claire. "Thank you," and she hurries across the street. The kids race to stick their hands in the bowl, each grab a fist full of cubes, bring it to their hot faces, necks, heads. In a few minutes, the last remnants lay melting on their would-be lawn. The kids, again, appear overheated and unhappy as they sit on the porch and begin to poke at one another until one or two complains and runs in the house.

"I wouldn't have given them ice had I known they were going to waste it like that. I thought they needed it," Sully scoffs.

Janet rolls her eyes.

At least the kids were happy for a moment, Rachel thought, but the moment didn't last.

Kyle raises his arms, pounding the heated air with his fists. "I am sick of this power outage. I didn't even see people over there working on it today. How are they going to get it fixed? I swear." His anger rises, as does his voice, "If they don't get this fixed, I am not paying my bill. I'm going to call them first thing..."

Suddenly the wasp flies in his face, taps his shoulder then retreats, hovering nearby.

Kyle jumps back, waves his arms madly. "Is it gone? Is it on me?" He spins, checks his shirt, and spins again.

The wasp remains subdued, hovering between him and the nest.

"Calm down," Rachel says. "She's over there."

"Damn." Sully searches the eaves. "Looks like you got a nest up there."

"Shit!" Kyle glances around the house, the porch.

"Better get rid of them," Janet offers. "Pretty soon, more will come. I've heard they nest into the thousands."

Rachel shakes her head, starts to say something when the kids react, "Wasps? Mom! Dad!"

"We gotta call someone. Oh Great! Our phones don't work."

"It's one wasp." Rachel attempts to be the voice of reason in the cacophony of rising anxiety.

"Well, it's one we can see," Kyle continues to inspect the house from his spot on the driveway. "The rest are probably in the walls or something."

"I've heard they can nest in the ground, wood piles. Much deadlier than bees," Sully says.

Rachel shakes her head, thinking of the natural insect control wasps provide, the pollination to gardens and flowers; a larger nest would be built elsewhere, out of sight of people or predators. She glances up at the nest and believes this little mother wasp is already considering a move. Too many people, too much noise, and far too much activity passing in the last day and a half for her to feel secure about this location.

Janet moves to the steps and sits down. Her face flushes, neck awash in crimson.

"Are they going to kill us?" Robbie backs into the door, closes the screen between him and his sister who reaches for the handle. They struggle for a moment before Robbie releases the door with a puckish grin.

Momma wasp hovers near her nest, observing the mélange of anxiety.

"I'm going to kill it before more come."

"She's just giving you a warning. You were too close to her nest," Rachel sits next to Janet and softly says, "You okay?"

"Honey, you know nothing about wasps." Kyle focuses on Sully. "Got any spray?"

"Adeara get Janet some ice water."

Adeara returns promptly and flanks her other side. "What's wrong?"

"Overheated, maybe." Janet takes a sip before placing the cold-sweating glass to her forehead.

"Hon, you okay?" Sully notices illness overtaking his wife. "I better get you home." He places his arm gently around her and, with Rachel on Janet's other side, begins home.

As Rachel returns, the buzz in the air grows. Everyone's windows are open, curtains stayed, even the birds and squirrels seem still from the heat. The street is a no man's land except for the rising sibilation.

Adeara waits for her mother on the patio. "Can I use your phone? I need to tweet something."

"You don't need..." Rachel's phone vibrates.

"Hello?... Oh no... That's terrible... Probably best..."

As she clicks off and slides the phone back into her pocket, Robbie joins them. "They called three urgent care centers. Two don't have power, third has people waiting on the sidewalk, Sully is taking Janet up north to a hospital."

"Why are the emergency rooms so busy?" Adeara moves closer to her mother.

Rachel shrugs and puts her arms around her kids. "Sick, overheated, accidents, I guess. Maybe just scared.

"Are we all going to get sick?" Robbie worries.

"No." Rachel pulls Robbie close to her. "No, honey. We just have to relax and stay cool. It'll be over..."

"Yeah, over soon." Kyle finishes the sentence with sarcasm.

"We're all a little on edge. Try to find a cool spot." She turns away from the invitation to argue and leads the kids inside.

Adeara opts for a cold shower and Robbie follows his dad to the garage.

Rachel closes the front door if only to shut out the low droning hum of the neighborhood. The whir of arguments, the swish of whining, and the vibration of uncomfortable family discussions usually hindered by the distractions of technology, hidden by the noise of the city, swirls on the street before it comes to rest like a misty layer of fog as the sun stretches out in the afternoon sky.

Rachel wakes in beads of sweat, her book on her chest, and the last streaks of sunlight pushing through the window of her bedroom. She stretches and moves slowly, refreshed from the impromptu but much needed nap. She emerges from her room to a house shadowed in evening light and Adeara eating peanut butter from the jar with a spoon.

"Really?" Rachel smiles as she reaches for a glass of water to rehydrate her sweaty body. Adeara shrugs in response. "Where's your dad and brother?"

"On a mission," she rolls her eyes, "to save us all from killer wasps."

Rachel jogs out the door. The garage door is open; the car in the driveway, and the keys abandoned on the patio. Kyle holds his arms up, spray can in one hand. "Done and done." Robbie's filming with his cellphone.

The rays of evening sun pinch Rachel's eyes. The murmur of the neighborhood hisses in her ears. The heat bears down as beads of sweat trickle down the front of her shirt. "You're an ass!" she yells. The only peaceful thing through this whole mess, a single mother building her nest.

"Oh, excuse me for saving our family. Those things are deadly." He matches her tone. "One sting and you're in the ICU. You want one of our kids in the hospital."

"Dad." Robbie's unheard as his cell still films.

"Really you two." Adeara watches from the doorway.

"You couldn't just leave her alone, could you!"

"You have been unbelievable during this whole disaster!"

"Kids, get in the car!" Rachel grabs the keys and heads for the car. "We'll be at my parents'."

Adeara jumps at the thought of air conditioning and falls in line behind her mother.

"But..." Robbie pauses, still looking through the viewfinder, and gazes around.

"Seriously!" Kyle steps away from the nest. "Now, you're going. We could have done that two days ago, but no. You and your 'it'll be over soon.'"

Their voices rose above the murmur, made the low whirring moans of unhappy family vibrate in tune with the buzz of the neighborhood.

"Kyle, you have been..."

The Wasp zips between them, flies around Kyle's head. Kyle drops the can of newly purchased wasp spray and waves his arms in panic. He spins, slapping at air, and twists back and forth. The wasp dips, lands instantaneously on the back of his pants, and disappears before Kyle screams in sudden searing pain.

He gasps, grabs his rear, "I'm stung. She stung me."

They're all at a standstill, catching up with the moment when Robbie says, "I tried to warn you, Dad." His phone still in hand.

Rachel's anger drains away. "Everyone in the car.

"You're leaving me like this?" Kyle howls.

"No." She shakes her head, "I'm taking you to the emergency room."

The kids start for the car, Kyle remains unmoving other than his hands rubbing his rear. "And wait four or five hours for treatment? No way."

"No?" All his gibbering about killer wasps.

"I'm not going to spend the whole night with a stinger in my rear in a waiting room for some doctor to charge me a thousand bucks to pull it out." He limps toward the patio.

A roar of televisions bleat to life, air conditioners whir, the violence of silence breaks as power surges through the electrical lines above. Neighbors' voices raise in a harmonious "hooray," and the quiet sigh of relief washes over all of them.

Adeara spins happily toward the house and disappears. Kyle limps up the first stair, "you coming?"

Rachel leans down and touches her hand on Robbie's shoulder, whispers, "did you get that?"

He smiles mischievously, races toward the house.

Rachel swings the keyring around her finger, glancing at Kyle. He winces, offers a sheepish grin. "I'll apologize for being a bum, if you bandage my bum."

"No swat team rescue needed?" She places her arm around his waist.

"You're never going to let me live this down, are you?"

"Not a chance." She gently pats his stung bum.

"Oww, owww."

The cool air curls around them as they enter; they notably relax as the even buzz of powered appliances quiet the rumbling of unhappy families.

How to Throw a Psychic a Surprise Party

"Coke, ecstasy, and pot," and without missing a breath, my daughter turned to me, "sorry, Mom."

I bit my lip to swallow a sob. She's embarrassed, yet sincere.

"Don't lie to me!" someone yelled in another room; our counselor stood and closed the door. It did little to muffle the sounds between rooms.

That, on our first visit here. This is our third or fourth.

We walk into this non-descript little building off University Circle. The guy in the front of the line whispers something we can't hear into the hole of the bullet proof glass.

"Sign in and sit down." The tiny receptionist's big voice booms throughout the lobby. No one glances up. The people are loud. They laugh and talk as two televisions bleat out reality shows.

When we step up, I pause. My daughter picks up the pen, hesitates. The woman behind the glass looks from me to her, senses our discomfort.

"Honey, fill out this form, step through that door." She points to the right.

We walk through the fog-glassed door into big blue room where little white daisies adorn the wall paper. We're cut off from the loud sounds, the rowdy feeling of the other waiting room. A single thirty-two inch Sony bolted to the wall airs a promo for the upcoming episode of Montel Williams, which features a psychic. I take the seat I took last time, two aisles over with my back to the door. This puts me in the center of the room where I can see the television, through the window to the patio, and the car park.

There seems some sort of calm in the empty space; I'm thankful. The chairs are lined up in rows, organized, quiet, unlike the other room where chaos reigns. The other reception room may hold half as many chairs, but there are twice as many people. It's all veiled by the wall, door, and by the petite woman who answers phones and barks orders. Once in a while, I hear her say, "sign in and sit down," in a tone I now suspect is reserved for regulars. Maybe, we have not yet become regulars. I want to believe we won't, but

I've lost count of how many times we've been here. As my daughter finishes the paperwork, I ask, "Is this the third time or the fourth time?"

Her face registers guilt; she shrugs, takes the paperwork up to the little window.

The lady's nice to her, "Go ahead, have a seat, hon. Someone will come get you."

Montel Williams welcomes his audience.

My daughter's eighteen; her mahogany hair and dark green eyes used to define her. Now it's the pale skin, the too thin frame, the lines forming around her eyes. When she was born and I saw those big, round eyes, I felt I'd known her forever. I felt then as I feel now, blessed. She graduated high school (barely) as an honor student (almost not), will attend University in the fall (hopefully).

The first time we came, she wanted me in the office with her. The counselor asked which drugs she used.

"That it?" The counselor, Ms. Rose, was a big woman with a gentle manner.

My first and only time in the room with Jade. There's only so much I can take.

Jade sits a few seats over. "Sorry, mom."

"For what?" I'm lost in my own meandering thoughts.

"Being here again."

"Better than not, right?" I speak carefully these days. I lean toward her, manage a smile that's stronger now. Because she's of age, my presence is not required, but her coming is a gift to me; my support, I hope, is so for her.

She returns the smile, turns her attention to the T.V. "What's this?"

The ghostly pale woman speaks to a specific audience member. "He wanted you to have something, a piece of jewelry. He wants to make certain you got it."

"A psychic," I answer.

A woman clad in red, hair in a ponytail, responds, "we found a ring in his bag."

"Yes, he says that's the one."

The audience releases a group sigh; the woman's eyes well with tears. "We were told it was his heart, but we thought his death might've been due to medication or…"

The psychic's head rolls like a bobble-head doll. "No, dear. Heart attack. He's grabbing his arm, pointing to his chest. He doesn't want you to worry. Your father wants you to be happy."

The woman begins to weep.

"You think this is real?" Jade stares at me with those intense green globes that appear bigger when she's gaunt, like now.

"Seems kind of general." I mimic the psychic. "Your sister was a woman, right? I'm sensing something bad happened to her."

Jade laughs, joins in. "She just got married!"

"Yes, I'm sensing her fear." I continue mocking.

"She's very happy!"

"I see that, but she had second thoughts."

"Who wouldn't?!" Jade snickers.

I'm happy we find humor even in moments like this; maybe, these days, it's only in moments like this. Our home is made of eggshells; navigating mood swings, highs, lows, clean, sober, my desire to push, hers to resist.

On television, the camera scans the audience before focusing on a young woman.

"Will I ever find the love of my life?" she asks.

The psychic rolls her head. "In the next two years."

"How does she know?" Jade's attention is rapt.

Jade's so young, too young, too little to deal with such a big problem.

"She said two years," I respond, "if you're searching for love, isn't there a good chance you'll find it within that time? It's not like she said next May 12."

"Oh yeah, huh."

The psychic says, "I see a D or a P, maybe an R, that's an initial."

Jade spins to me.

I offer, "how many names begin with or contain one of those letters? Or, she'll say, it's a family name or company name."

"It could be the company he works for, or..." the psychic continues.

A sly smile plays on Jade's mouth. "You're pretty good at this."

I'm pleased she's impressed; but, I also have to admit, it's the thousand and one promises from her that allows me to see through the empty words of others. I've become a human lie detector. It's a different world when naiveté fades.

Jade hunches her shoulders, shivers, leans forward.

"They're going to give the psychic a surprise party at the end of the show."

Her eyes widen. "How do you know?"

"Previews," I laugh more loudly than intended.

She laughs too.

For a moment, we are mother and daughter, not enabler and addict.

The door squeaks open, a woman pokes her head in, "Jade?"

"Uhm, you can wait here, okay?"

"Oh yeah." There are some things a mother doesn't want to hear, especially more than once.

"Hey, Jade." I call after her.

"Yeah?"

"How do you throw a psychic a surprise party?"

"I don't ... oh, I get it. Yeah, right!"

Jade disappears. I survey the outside. Some of the regulars made their way to the only trash container with an ashtray; they pass the door, stand, smoke. More cars arrive, none have left. This place deceives from the outside; it's small, inconspicuous. Hidden like a secret.

I give my attention back to the psychic. On the screen, a man steps up, mid-forties, gray hairs in his five o'clock shadow. "My grandma passed rather suddenly..."

If the psychic warned me one day I'd be here, I wouldn't't've believed her. Sometimes, I wish someone had told me, her friends, a teacher, but I wouldn't have trusted their word. I didn't have faith in the first counselor, three or four visits ago, when she told me we were in for a long, hard ride. I didn't listen to the next counselor, a year later, when she said to leave Jade in rehab for the holidays.

I'm not certain of much anymore. No prayers answered, no therapy has worked, and every time Jade says, even tries to mean, "this will be the last time," I don't have the heart to believe her, but I hope. The last time we came here, the counselor said, "it'll get worse before it gets better." That, I assume, is fact.

"Oh, honey, your grandma wants you to know she is at peace now. She's telling me she left you something."

"She did." His voice lifts; his eyes shine.

The counselor called this a disease. At first, I thought, if this were a disease, the insurance would cover the care, I'd have support, this would have brought her father and I closer, not tear us apart. But, now, many visits later, I understand it is a disease. An isolating and lonely disease.

My attention drifts as I hear the receptionist's voice soften. "Go through there, fill out this form."

When I refocus on the thirty-two inch screen, Montel brings out the cake for the surprise party; for a moment, the psychic's persona slips down. Surprise surrounds her eyes, her lips turn up in response. Maybe not everyone sees it, but I do. Then, just as quickly, she plays the clairvoyant, presses her lips together, closes her eyes to replace the surprise with humble acknowledgement.

A family walks in, moves to the same row where I sit, but further down: mom, dad, son. Mom appears stressed, short uncombed hair, bags under her eyes. Her hand shakes as she reaches into her purse. The mom sits with her back to the patio, the boy across from her. He must be sixteen.

Dad wears a suit, paces, scrutinizes the boy. "You missed one." He points to the paper.

"I don't know what to put there." The boy's voice, defiant.

I see the father through my peripheral as he walks away, paces back; he notices me.

A counselor pushes the door open, "Come on back."

"I haven't finished." The boy's spine stiffens; he doesn't want to be here.

"You can finish in here." The counselor is a man, experienced, unsmiling.

The boy gets up, focuses on his dad, "Can you wait here?"

Dad shakes his head no.

The counselor directs his hard stare at the father. "I'll call you when I need you."

Perhaps the counselor understands what I've come to intuit and what his parents can't yet: the boy's not ready to be here, and the father's not helping the situation.

At least, this visit was Jade's idea. Hope washes over me. It's fool's gold here.

The father drops his body down a few seats over from his wife. "We won't have this, no sirree, not at all." He says it more for my sake than his wife's.

She stands, "I need some air," heads outside to the patio. His eyes follow her until the door closes, then he sits back in the chair. She gazes back, can't see through the greyed-privacy windows.

I watch his wife bum a cigarette from one of the regulars, puff on it like her life depends on it.

His eyes are on the floor. "This doesn't happen in families like ours," he announces.

I used to think the same thing.

"Just hanging out with the wrong people!" He bounces his foot on the floor.

I don't look over. At one time, I thought similarly.

"He'll overcome, got a will of iron." His fist pounds softly on the wooden arm of the chair.

I twist back to the door the kids went through. Once I was convinced it was simply willpower.

Those thoughts, naive. Understanding comes harder.

"My wife and I both used to smoke. We woke up one morning, said enough is enough, stopped right then and there."

I recognize there's hope in his voice as my attention curls to the window; his wife stubs out the cigarette on the handrail, tosses it in the trash. He follows my gaze but just misses the scene.

On T.V., Montel cuts the cake, passes a piece to the pale woman who smiles.

"Is this your first time here?" The father's voice softens.

Montel and the audience begin to sing, "Happy Birthday to you..."

He notices the television. "What is this?"

"They've thrown the psychic a party."

He slaps the chair's arm, "Damn psychics, what do they know?"

"What do any of us really know?" I respond softly.

I watch the happy, hopeful faces of the television audience eat cake. The camera pans on the woman who asked about her father, the man who asked about a grandmother, the young woman looking for love. It hits me – hope. The psychic isn't working with unknown forces, but with the mysterious powers of empathy. People don't come to her to find out that someone is going to die or if their kid is on drugs, they come to her after, just to hear someone say that everything is going to be okay.

All the visits, the warnings I received; they were sympathetic, but they weren't hopeful. I didn't understand then. I couldn't hear the message.

The father straightens up, shifts toward me; before he says anything, I answer his first question.

"No, this is not our first time here."

He looks at me a little confused.

The sounds from the next room seep in. The receptionist yells, "Keep it down! This isn't a roadhouse!"

"This place is pure chaos," he says. "It sounds like a damn party over there."

His wife bums another cigarette and I realize they have difficult years ahead of them.

Montel raises the cake in toast to the psychic, all the happy smiling faces following along. Their problems have not been solved, they still have a dead father, a grandmother who passed, and a lonely bed to sleep in tonight, but they're celebrating.

The father watches me, waits for some sort of confirmation or acknowledgement. I want to tell him to strap in, he's in for a roller coaster of a ride. But he's not in a place to hear that. And it's not what he needs either. I offer a warm smile, "it's going to be okay."

"What's that?"

"Everything," I glance from the television to him. "It'll all work out. Your son, and all, he'll be okay."

His foot stops bouncing. He glances around the room, turns to the window and notices his wife stubbing out a cigarette on the patio before heading back in.

I stand up, move toward the other room. He's the one who needs the private room now; maybe I need the party.

I open the door; the reverberations of chaos pour in. The receptionist appears surprised as I step into the lobby.

"Tell my daughter, I'll be over here."

The corners of her mouth lift upward in a small but perceptive smile; she nods.

The door closes behind me. The televisions drown each other out. The people laugh loudly, move the chairs to suit themselves, and talk at full volume about nothing very important.

Bowie and the Basket Case

After I was robbed, I kept missing random
things. Things a good thief would never take,
like my Bowie t-shirt. But I was certain, since I
couldn't find it, it must've been stolen. Then, in
another week or so, I'd find it in some obscure
place. My Coffeeology mug under the sink; my
Mac Honeylove lipstick in the cookie jar. My
mind filled with dark thoughts; maybe
someone's toying with me.

"Do you think the person could be coming
back?" I call the number on the card the officers
left and ask one of them.

He exhales a heavy breath as if he wants me to
hear it through the phone. "Ma'am, we don't
usually find thieves come back unless it's for
something of value."

"Of course, of course." I realize how paranoid this sounds so I never say it aloud again. I imagine they grew tired of me calling and saying, I think something else is missing.

"Just make a list and drop it off in a few weeks." I recognize the resigned tone of Officer Cardonas from the night he and his partner took my report. I feel like he eighty-sixes my paperwork as we speak, and I wish I remembered the younger officers name. He had, at least, hid his annoyance.

I'm surprised anyone broke in at all. It's not like I have much. The house is a small rental in a mediocre neighborhood. The once green paint is peeling in strips on the exterior, screens missing from the windows, dry patches of brown next to bushy overgrown weeds. It's not a house that screams there's something of value here. The thieves lifted the DVD player, a few dollars in change, and a pair of earrings that I didn't care about anyway. They even left the Magnavox.

"I wonder why they didn't take that," I mentioned as we did the walk-thru.

The officers chuckled.

The younger officer, whose name escapes me, covered his chuckle with a cough as he spoke. "They want stuff they can sell fast."

"Are those rabbit ears?" I heard Cardonas whisper as they continued walking through the house.

"Anything else of value that you might be missing? Cash, jewelry?"

I shrugged. "I don't really keep cash, except what I pull out of my clothes on laundry day. Maybe four bucks in change." I use it to treat myself when I'm feeling down on one of those long, lonely weekends. I scoop it out of the little tin dish and take myself out for a frozen yogurt or Frappuccino.

Officer Cardonas handed me the lined sheet of paper. "List everything you feel is missing, drop this off at the station as soon as you can. Keep a copy for your insurance company." He dropped his eyes and released his resigned breath as if it wouldn't make a difference whether I dropped it off or not.

I suppose it's not what the thieves took, it's what they left; a lingering anxiety that I'd been invaded. The thieves rifled through my personal things, and they might've taken things I hadn't yet discovered.

The fear they might return dissipated. I told myself, there's nothing more they'd want. Besides paying for a thicker, heavy back door to be installed, I dont bother to replace the items they stole. I can't afford an alarm system, and I'm uncomfortable with the idea of a security company having access to cameras they'd place in my house.

When I report to work late the next day, I explain to Leonard, the manager, and show him the paperwork for the new door. I work in the front office of a large furniture distributor. This makes me one of several customer service agents. In short, I answer phones. I can't say I'm popular at the office. I'm not a pariah, but no one tries to get to know me. Some of the ladies go out to lunch together. They've invited me once or twice, but maybe it's because I bring a sandwich that they don't ask often. However, by the time I get to my desk, word of the break-in has spread and people go out of their way to talk to me. Nancy, the girl who sits next to me, leans over and whispers, "Anna, my break's at ten. Take yours then too."

Another woman who brings me files, offers, "I heard. So sorry."

Someone from human resources brings me coffee. "Are you sure you don't need a day off? Maybe, you should go home, rest, relax."

I decline. The thought of being home alone during the day, when the burglars broke in, scares me.

The breakroom is relatively small. The company doesn't want us loitering and gossiping. There's a coffee pot and a single table with a few chairs. When the microwave broke, they didn't bother to buy a new one. But, at break, several office-mates gather around to hear my story.

"After work, I walked in and saw the house was a mess. They'd broken in through the back door."

"Did you check all the windows, in case they left one unlocked to come back?" Nancy asks.

That scares the hell out of me.

"Check your closets," Monica, from payroll, offers.

"Check your bank accounts, in case they stole your identity." Jenny's the administrative assistance; she's never in here.

All these things I hadn't considered. It's helpful, but also terrifying.

I'm torn that night. I don't want to go home, but know I need to check the closets and windows preferably before dark. I go to dinner and linger at the table, then make it home right before dusk. I leave the front door open and pretend to call out to a friend, "Jake, I'll be right out."

I live in a one bedroom with a den and a small bathroom. I can stand in the dining room and see almost every room, but I carry my cell phone in my hand as I walk through the house; as if anyone jumped out I'd actually have the wherewithal or even the time to call the police. When I'm sure it's safe, I close the front door.

Since I no longer own a DVD player, I watch an old *Three's Company* rerun. Jack is in a flower shop when they are held up by a thief with a gun. I turn it off mid-show. What if my burglars had a gun? What if they come back with a gun? I walk around the house checking the door and window locks, close the curtains. I replay the conversation with the police after I asked about the TV. I can't imagine the burglars would come back with a gun. It's not like I have anything.

When I call my insurance agent the next morning from the break room, she says in a faux-sweet tone, "You have a thousand-dollar co-pay. Did they take a thousand dollars' worth of stuff?"

"No."

"No use making a claim." She sounds unconcerned that I've been invaded, that things are missing. And she certainly doesn't seem to care if I have only reruns on basic cable to watch.

"Lie," Nancy whispers as she pours her coffee and sits at the table next to me. She stuffs dried apricots into her mouth as she adds, "Tell them they took more jewelry or your grandma's heirloom whatever."

"I already gave the list to the police."

"Give them another list, tell 'em you just noticed." She sucks down her coffee in a hurry to get as much refreshment in our ten-minute break as possible. We aren't to have food or drink at our desks; this is our only chance to eat or drink before lunch. I usually just have a glass of water.

Monica, from payroll, overhears us as she enters. "I wouldn't. You need receipts or pictures." She pours herself a cup of coffee and sips as if she has all the time in the world. Her department is nowhere near as strict as the customer service department.

"You can get pictures. You can manufacture receipts." Nancy slurps the last of the coffee and wipes her hands on a napkin. "Lunch?" she asks as we head back to our desks.

"Lunch," Monica responds as if it's all been decided.

Nancy, Monica, and I are joined by a few other ladies. All through our In-N-Out Double-Doubles, they ask more questions about the break in: what did they take? did I check this or that? and so on.

I can't say I've become popular, but I've made friends. We talk on breaks, go out to lunch, and sometimes we go out for drinks after work. When we don't go out together, I don't feel safe enough to be alone, so I go to the shops. Then I repeat the whole spectacle every night: leave the front door open, check the house, then shut and lock the door.

Monica volunteers at an animal shelter on weekends as she's unmarried and doesn't have much family. She says it gives her something to do and makes her feel valuable. She asks me to come with one day; the rescue sponsors adoption days at local pet supply stores and needs extra help. On Saturday, we bring dogs out of their cages and place them in make-shift puppy play-pens; the cats stay in their cages, no pens for them. Then we sit in front of the store in the steamy spring weather.

Random people stop to ask questions, talk, or just pet the puppies or kittens. Monica told me earlier that if they ask about the animal to just make up what I thought they wanted to hear. At first I don't offer much but, if I make something up, they're more likely to adopt the animal or donate money to the rescue.

"What kind of dog is this?" A woman with two children pauses in front of one of the puppy playpens. She's tall in her three-inch heels and carries a Versace purse. She doesn't seem the type to purchase a rescue dog. Her children just want to play with them. I don't even see which dog she points to, but I start talking.

"That little pup is a mix."

"A mix of what?" She reaches over and pats one of the dogs. These dogs are dumped, found, surrendered, so the rescue rarely has any type of background on the animals. This little guy looks part Jack Russel Terrier to me, but she's not the type to appreciate an excited animal.

"Well, we believe he's part terrier and part hound dog. That means is that he will be playful enough with the kids, but he won't become too excited because hounds are notoriously mellow."

She seems to like that description. "Will he make a good watch dog?"

"The terrier part of him will. They are naturally protective of their families and he will alert you to anyone around your home." I assume this to be true since terriers bark a lot.

After the "please, mom, please" subsides, she takes the dog inside and pays the rescue fee, even donating extra money for food and shots for the unadopted critters. I smile as I watch her through the window. It feels good to give these dogs a home, so they won't have to spend one more night caged in a lonely kennel.

A man's laugh startles me. "You just made that up."

I turn to see a thin, relatively young man smirking at me; he has blonde curly hair covered by a baseball cap and dark sunglasses hide his eyes.

"Did I say something wrong? Terriers do bark. Hounds are mellow," I reason.

He smiles and nods. "Okay, you got me." Then he walks by without even bending down to pet a dog or put his finger in one of the cat cages.

But, I do notice, as he walks away, that he wears an older, black Bowie concert t-shirt remarkably like the one I'm unable to find. I questioned myself when I noticed it missing: Had I donated it? Used it to clean my car? But seeing one on him, I remember it's in my pajama drawer. It wasn't nice enough to wear out anymore, and its long sleeves and thick fabric make a perfect bedtime tee on chilly nights.

I sift through my pj's that night. No luck.

A week later, after happy hour with the ladies from the rescue, I feel comfortable coming home. I don't check every room, and I stroll in like I used to. Usually I do laundry on Saturday mornings, but since I've been spending more time outside of my little home with people from work and the rescue, laundry and cleaning are relegated to whenever I have time.

I gather the laundry from the bedroom, the bathroom, a random sweater left on the chair in the dining room, socks on the living room floor. I wash dishes while the laundry runs, then I sweep the floor. Not much of a Saturday night, but productive enough. When all is done, I pull the single load of laundry from the dryer and fold it. I freeze. My Bowie t-shirt! I stand there staring at it without word or thought for the longest time. Had I been mistaken? Had it been stuck in the bottom of the basket? Static-trapped between two other things?

A creepy, spidery feeling climbs over my shoulders as if someone stood behind me. I spin around. Of course, no one's there. I ran through the house, checking doors, windows, closets, even under my darn bed and behind the couch. I recheck the doors. Then I come back to face Bowie. "Where have you been?" As if the shirt could tell me a story.

"Okay, okay," I say aloud to myself as if that could break the uneasy feeling sniggling up my spine.

On Monday at work, I mention the mysterious disappearance/reappearance over lunch. The ladies don't pick up on it. They ignore it and change the topic. I bring it up again, "I swear, I couldn't find it, then suddenly, boom."

"Oh, geez Anna, it happens all the time," Monica says without looking at me.

"Socks," Nancy announces while finishing her salad as if in a hurry again. "All the time. Dryer. Disappear. Reappear."

"My repair guy pulled a pair of my Victoria's Secret panties out of my washer motor. Said to use lingerie bags," says Donna from human resources. "I was so embarrassed. But they were ruined. Had to throw them away."

Then they change the topic to something else.

The whole conversation, their lack of empathy for my fear and confusion makes me want to leave. So, after work, no errands, no dinner out, and when they ask me later that week to happy hour, I refuse. I want to hermitize in my house.

The evening is quiet and breezy in my little neighborhood. I go to bed early, but I'm not tired; I'm bored. I reach into my bedside table to retrieve my journal, figure I'll catch up on some thoughts. But it's not there. I'm slack on keeping it. It's not something that I write in every night, maybe a once a week, sometimes more or less depending on what's happening in my life. Overall, it's a pretty boring read. I try to remember when I wrote in it last. I remember writing about the women I work with.

My nightstand lamp is still on, but I get up and flip the switch for the overhead. I search the little table thoroughly, look underneath, behind, slide the drawer out. I wonder if I left it in another room, so I hunt through the living room; there have been maybe two or three occasions I wrote in it while sitting on the couch, but it's unlikely I left it out. I move the sofa, overturn the cushions. I leave the living room and go back to my bedroom, open the drawers of my dresser, swing open the closet doors, nearly climb under my own bed. As a teenager, I'd hidden my journal between the mattress and box spring, not that there was anything risky in it then either. However, this journal is my adult journal. I wrote about the men I dated -in detail. I wrote about my family, my coworkers. Sometimes still I write silly and stupid musings of a girl who never grew up.

Of everything I'm convinced the thieves stole, all the useless list of items that I wrote down, then found later: Garlic press. Gloves. Bowie t-shirt. I'm unconvinced that they took my journal. And my biggest fear is that they did.

I barely sleep; I fall into a restless, sickening type of doze about five a.m., miss my alarm at seven and hightail it to work an hour late. It's been a few months since the robbery, but they're not buying that it's break-in after-effects. I don't tell them my journal is missing. I explain I felt fearful and couldn't sleep. The ladies walk away, as if I'm asking for special attention; my boss, Leonard, runs his hand over the few strands of hair he has left. He does this when he's annoyed. I'm unfocused most of the day, have trouble getting the messages right and answering questions that I mindlessly respond to every day.

At the end of the day, my boss calls me to his office. "Anna, you've used this robbery as an excuse long enough."

I stand silent. My mouth might've fallen open if I hadn't clenched my teeth.

"That's all anyone hears around here. Honey, people get robbed all the time."

I want to defend that it's all anyone asks me about, that I don't go around volunteering information.

"Now, not one more thing about this robbery. Okay?" Although he attempting to be empathetic, Leonard's an asshole.

At lunch the following day, Donna inquires, "Do you have an extra key at home that they could have taken?" Without time to answer, she adds, "You should get a dog."

Monica turns back. "Yes, the event this Saturday."

Maybe I'm a little paranoid, but I wonder if they know something I don't. I question if they laugh about my missing/found items like my Bowie shirt behind my back or even somehow got a peek at my dairy pages.

One of them could've said something to Leonard about the burglary conversations because they'd read something about themselves they didn't like in my journal. I wrote about the way Nancy eats everything like it's her last meal and how Donna never makes eye contact with the person she's talking to. Someone complained to Leonard. He's never around when we're talking. Are they getting pleasure from reading my stories of bad dates, mother issues, and loneliness? Or some sick satisfaction listening to me freak out about some random missing item, then freak out again when it magically reappears?

I remain quiet for the rest of lunch. Later that week, when they ask me out for drinks after work, I make an excuse. I search everywhere for my journal, the other rooms, the bathroom, the kitchen. I even dive through the laundry basket. I want to believe it's misplaced so I can dispense with the paranoid storyline running through my head.

My house appears much worse than when I was robbed. I tell myself I'll put it back together the next day. Another sleepless night, and I drag myself through work the next day. I decline lunch and happy hour, saying I'm too tired.

Monica declares as we're leaving work, "Remember, adoption event tomorrow."

"I can't," I try to think of a random excuse. "My mom," is all I come up with.

"Honey, we need you," Monica whines. "And I got the perfect little boy for you. I've been holding on to him all week because I thought you'd like him. Perfect watch dog, but mellow enough that he can be kept in at night."

I turn away and roll my eyes. "Okay."

That night I shop at the market. As I pick over the apples, the produce man who's never even glanced at me stands there staring. When I look at him, wondering why he's watching me, he moves nearer and asks, "Is there anything I can help you with?"

I've shopped at the store for three years. He's never said anything to me. It feels too personal. I think about my missing journal, say, "no, thank you," and scurry away. In the freezer section, there are a lot of strange men picking out pizzas and burritos, and it feels like they too are observing me with too much interest.

I tell myself I'm imagining things but still rush to the cashier.

"How are you?" The lady is my mom's age. She's worked there for years. She's sweet but more talkative than most.

"Good," I say.

"Really? I don't know." She studies me instead of ringing my groceries.

"I'm in a hurry." I glance at the food on the conveyor belt.

She snorts. "I doubt that."

I wonder what she means. It's Friday night. Isn't everyone here on a Friday night in a hurry to go somewhere, if even home?

"I have a date," I blurt out, stupidly.

"Okay," she sniffs.

One of my last diary entries was about how I never seem to have a date on Friday nights. Let's say, it's been a dry season. A very long, very dry season.

As I drive home, I wonder if whoever has taken my journal is sharing it. The police said the thief probably watched the house, knew my schedule. Could be a neighbor. Maybe they're spreading rumors or, worse, it's on the internet. There's a neighborhood watch site. Are pages of my journal hiding among the posts I never read? I sit on my disheveled couch and eat a microwave dinner while watching *Golden Girls*.

On Saturday, the pet adoption is held at the mall. I feel exposed, as if everyone who walks by knows some intimate secret of mine. I know it's silly. And I tell myself this. I don't make as much conversation, don't lie to get a critter adopted. I let Monica do the talking and, when she walks away, I offer, "We don't actually have a background."

Monica brings out a little dog. "This is Irving. And I think you two are perfect for one another." She presents this black and tan pooch that appears to be somewhere between a chihuahua and a miniature border collie. It has short, soft fur and a thin body.

"I think getting a dog is a bit premature." I try to refuse.

"Are you kidding? I'd say it's a bit too late. But if they do come back, this guy will be ready."

He certainly is cute. "He'll be alone all day."

"Exactly what you need! To keep strangers and burglars away."

"He doesn't really look big enough to do any damage."

"He doesn't have to be big! When thieves hear a dog, they go find someone else's house to break into." She's not letting up.

Monica sets Irving on my lap and skips over to a young girl eyeing the cat cate. I pat his head, hoping someone else will come by and fall in love with him.

"Is this guy up for adoption?" A man with short hair and thick glasses pauses next to the little dog.

"Yeah. Well, no. I guess not."

The dog hums a low growl.

The young man chuckles, "Can't decide?"

"Well, someone picked him out for me. I haven't decided…" I look up at this stranger. He's familiar for some reason. I tilt my head and try to remember. Maybe other adoption events.

Irving growls louder, begins to bark. I hold him tighter.

"Well, it'll keep you from being lonely on those long weekends."

His voice trails off as he walks away, but the words echo in my head. That is, almost word for word, what I wrote down in my journal on my last three-day weekend: I wish I had something to keep me from being lonely on these long weekends. I snap my head up, watch him walk away. The guy, for some reason, reminds me of the young man wearing that Bowie shirt. I don't know if it's the hair, the jeans, or the slow saunter as he slinks away.

"Hey," I call after him. But the dog jumps and barks in his direction.

As we're packing it up for the day, I tell Monica, "This is my last day." She whines and asks me to stay, but I tell her there are family issues.

She's single, has three dogs, a cat, and a rabbit. The other volunteers are mostly single and have multiple animals too. There seems to be a uniformity here that I don't want to be equated with. However, they all insist, they've never been robbed. Irving might act as a good deterrent for returning thieves, but I don't want to end up with a menagerie.

Coming home from work to be greeted by Irving's wagging tail somehow relieves the fear. I feel better, like the house is safe and protected. Irving barks if anyone comes close to the house or knocks on the door, but he doesn't yap obnoxiously.

Spending evenings with Irving lifts the loneliness and boredom. Even just sitting there petting him while watching those *Three's Company* episodes makes the show funnier. When I walk him, the neighbors say hello or let him play with their dogs. I look forward to coming home.

I even stop worrying about my journal – mostly.

On Friday, excited about the evening walk with Irving, I throw open door. For the first time, Irving's not waiting there.

"Irving?" I call. "Walk?" I bait.

No clicking paws across the living room floor. No puppy whine from the other room.

"Irving!" I call louder.

Not a bark, not a whimper. I step in without fear, look from room to room. Is he stuck under the bed? Somehow shut himself in a closet?

"Irving?"

When I come to the back door, it's open. Not wide open, just a little. I worry he's gotten out. I pull the door wide. "Irving!"

My next-door neighbor stretches up over the block wall. "What's wrong, Anna?"

"I can't find Irving." Soon she's calling for him and some of the neighbors help me search. We can't find him anywhere. It's not yet dark outside when, in tears, I retreat to my house and phone the police.

"My dog's missing," I sniffle.

"I think you need the ASPCA," the lady's monotone borders on annoyance.

"No. No. Someone broke in. Well, I think. The door was open." My voice shakes. I'm more concerned for the little dog than I am that someone invaded my privacy again.

A police car arrives, and it's the same two officers as the first time. Their faces betray their thoughts as they approach the door.

I explain, show them the back door.

"Are you sure," asks officer Cardonas, "that you just didn't leave the door open."

"No." I snark at him. "I would not have left the door open because I have been robbed and because every time I call you guys, you treat me like I'm making things up."

The younger officer, his badge reads Del Rio, pats Cadonas' shoulder and takes over. He inspects the door. It hasn't been broken in, but the lock is scratched up. "May have picked the lock." He steps outside in the yard, walks over into the grass.

"All my neighbors helped me search. I don't know, I think…"

"Valuable dog?" He walks around the yard.

I shake my head. "Rescue."

"I'm not sure there's much…" He leans over into the weeds, picks something up. He inspects the wall more closely. "Looks like we got some blood here."

"Blood?!"

He turns around, seems regretful he said it aloud. He makes his way back toward me and holds out his gloved hand. "Is this yours?"

"My journal!" I grab it from his hand and hold it to my chest. Tears form. "I tried to tell you." I cry. "Someone's been coming back here. First one thing was missing, then I'd find that and something else…"

He places his hand on my arm to calm me, to lead me back into the house. Officer Del Rio speaks quietly to his partner while I look through the pages of my dirtied journal as if trying to make certain all my secrets are still there.

"We're going to get some crime scene techs out here. They won't be here until tomorrow," he says while Cardonas steps outside and unclips the radio from his belt.

"I'm going to close the door. I don't want you to touch it or open it until the team has a chance to fingerprint it. What else do you think might have been disturbed?"

I walk quickly from room to room. "I just came home, and the dog, my dog Irving and so I went..." I realize I'm muttering, but I can't help it.

Officer Del Rio leads me to the couch, urges me to sit down, "Okay, Ma'am. We'll find your dog."

He's lying. Officers do not take time out of their busy schedules to look for little rescue puppies. "Anna," I say, not looking at him.

"Pardon me?" He leans down. He smells musky-clean, like argon and tea tree oil. I wonder if it's his shampoo or his after shave.

"Anna," I repeat. "I don't like Ma'am. My mother is a ma'am. My grandmother is a ma'am."

He smiles. "My apologies, Anna. I'm James. We're going to do everything we can."

I look into his eyes. I don't believe him..

I take my journal to bed with me that night, start to open it, but I put it aside. It doesn't feel like mine anymore. It feels foreign, violated.

I like awake but motionless most of the night. At some point, I stumble to the bathroom to wipe my runny nose when I hear a rustling. I pause, suck in air so quickly that I gag. I hear the sound again, flip on the light.

The laundry basket shimmies slightly. Tissue in my hand, I step closer. The smallest little whine escapes the wicker basket.

"Irving?" I bolt across the chilled floor and flip open the top. The black-and-tan-bigger-than-a-chihuahua mix jumps up and squeaks.

"Irving!" I pick up his wiggling little happy body. "What were you doing in there?" He makes throaty sounds and tries to lick my face. I hug him.

In the morning, a knock on the door inspires Irving to tear through the house for a good bark. When I open it, he sits at attention.

"You found your dog?" The officer, James Del Rio, in a t-shirt and jeans, smiles at us.

I almost don't recognize him. "Yeah, he was hiding in the laundry basket."

"Oh, good. I came to help you look, but…" He stands there looking through the screen at the dog. "Well, you were missed."

At a loss for what else to do, I open the door for the officer and invite him in. Irving wags his tail and jumps on him excitedly.

"I have good news." He picks up Irving. "Is he always this friendly?"

"I guess." I chuckle and think, I don't usually have guests. "Good news?"

"After we left, I called the local emergency rooms and told them to let me know if someone came in with a dog bite." He puts Irving down and follows me into the kitchen.

"Coffee?" My cup sits half full on the counter.

"Yes, thanks. And, well, I got a call."

"Really? Already?" I open the cabinet and retrieve another cup for him as he grabs the coffee pot and fills both cups.

"I went down, questioned him. Milk?"

I point to the fridge. "And?"

"And... well, we're holding him at the station pending an I.D. How do you feel about going for a line-up?"

"But I never saw him."

He returns the milk to the refrigerator and hands me my cup as he takes the other and sips from it. "I don't want to frighten you, but he claims you two are friends."

My back stiffens and my breath catches in my throat.

"He won't be able to see you; it's one-way glass."

James drives me to the police station in his own car. He's officially off duty and doesn't need to do this. "It seems he's done this before. He does, in some way, interact with his victims. If they work at a supermarket, he stops to buy groceries, drops little hints, wears a hat he took or..."

"A shirt," I finish his statement. I remember a man in a Bowie shirt, but don't know if I'd recognize him.

At the station, James leads me into an observation room as another detective questions the young man on the other side of the glass. "Do you recognize him?"

I step closer to the glass. Curly hair, thin. He looks familiar. James clicks a switch on the wall, and I hear his voice. "She's kinda lonely. She doesn't interact with people much."

Instantly, it comes to me. He talked to me at the mall. Irving growled at him then. He was at the other adoption event too. My Bowie shirt now feels vile; I want to throw it away the moment I get home!

"You remember?"

"The pet adoptions."

James nods. "Yeah, it's not about stealing; he likes taunting his victims."

A chill sweeps through me. "Sick."

"She's not much of a joiner. And beyond that, she doesn't let people in. I told her..." He's trying to convince them that he knows me, as if we're friends. That creepy feeling crawls into my shoulders, under my arms, and it encloses my chest.

"He has a type. He picks women who are unmarried, who may or may not have many friends. We're not sure how he focuses in on them."

I'm a "type," I think. And Officer James Del Rio is being nice; what he really means is "may not have friends."

"He's never been convicted."

"Why not?" I step back, my hands grasping at my blouse. I know I should feel safer since he's in police custody, and they don't believe one thing he's telling them, but something about what he is saying hits me – the stranger-stalker seems to have put his finger on some very real things about me. The sides of my mouth drag down and I taste a hint of vomit in my mouth.

"Anna," he says, "honestly, it's the journals. He takes the lady's diary. Most women are too... ah... well... I don't know, embarrassed, afraid, whatever, to have that turned over into evidence, to have it possibly read in a court of law. Also, he's tells the women he's made copies to be released on the internet. We don't think that's true, but most women don't want to take that chance."

The thought of my diary, my private thoughts, out for public consumption makes me want to shrink into my very own laundry basket. I'm backing up, wrapping my arms around myself, as if I'm already closing that wicker lid on top of myself.

James knows I've connected the ideas. He opens the door and half-smiles. "Let me take you home. I'm sure you want to get some rest."

The drive home is quiet. Using y journal as evidence is not the only thing making me uncomfortable; the creep read something in there which can't be argued with. He might be a basket case, but I have my own issues. I consider the ladies at work. I've interacted with them, but it was only lately we became friendly. Then, I pulled back from that too. I bite my lip and watch the streets pass us by as I realize I need to make some changes.

When we arrive at my house, James walks me up to the door. "I'll wait while you make sure everything okay," he says with a sense of defeat; he's been through this before with other victims, that is clear.

I open the door and Irving isn't there. I call, but he doesn't come.

James steps closer to the door. "Where is he?" He follows me in. "Where'd you find him last night?"

I walk toward the bathroom with James close behind me. I open the lid of the laundry basket and Irving is there, shaking. When he sees us, he starts wagging his tail.

"Aww, he's scared." James reaches down to pick him up. Irving licks his hand, wiggles in his arms and tries to lick his face.

"Hey, Little Boy, is that your hiding space?" James nuzzles Irving while he walks back toward the living room.

"I'll be right back." In a moment, I return with that dirtied, invaded journal. I hand him the diary and take Irving.

"Convict that guy. I don't care what happens. How dare he scare my poor little pup like that."

A slow smile rises across his jaw. "Are you sure?" He pulls a glove from a pocket to cover the diary, taking it carefully.

I nod. "Well," I half-heartedly smile. "My life is pretty boring." Mostly, it is. But, still, private thoughts, physical descriptions. I cringe to think of what people might think of it. Maybe they'll come to the same conclusions that creep did. Maybe the people I wrote about, my parents and my co-workers, will all hate me. I pull Irving close to me and put my cheek on his soft fur. But that horrible man who invades people's home and scares their dogs has to be stopped.

"The forensic team will be out later today. With this journal and the results from their investigation, I think we've got him." He pauses, closes my screen door as he looks through it. "Just to let you know, I don't have any reason to read this."

I release a breath I didn't know I was holding. There's a lot I'm going to have to own up to, and maybe it's about time.

I lock the screen door as James shuffles down the steps. "Maybe, I could come back and visit Irving. I've worked with dogs before, maybe we can make him comfortable again."

I think he might mean he's worked with victims, but I'll take his words at face value. And Irving smells musky, clean like argon and tea-tree oil with a touch of doggie breath. "We'd like that." It's a nice scent, all mixed together.

After I close the door, I march to my bedroom and pull that violated Bowie shirt out of my pajama drawer. I take the tee and Irving out to the living room and set them both down. "Get it, boy," I say. "Tear it up."

Irving cocks his head, sniffs the shirt, and growls before he goes crazy on it. I sit back on my couch and think, we're going to be just fine.

Friends, Lovers, and Liars

My friends trust me with their secrets; they believe they're receiving honest, unfettered advice from a moral, upstanding citizen. So I don't share my new lifestyle.

My mother brags to friends how I am her most honest child. "Leona doesn't lie about her weight or her age or her natural hair-color." As if anyone cares about those things. And she defends me ardently.

At Sunday brunch, when the waiter jokingly questions my honesty about my caffeine intake, her aged, cracked voice raises, "why would she lie about coffee?!" Her small frame barely takes up the chair, but her voice carries throughout the restaurant.

"Mom, it doesn't matter. It was a joke." I try to calm her.

"I don't care, g'damnit!" The anger twists her face; offense resonates in her tone.

The waiter catches my eye, smiles knowingly, and says, "my apologies ma'am, I meant no offense," before walking away.

He knows I lie. Some men can tell. Not that I lie about caffeine intake, but about my loyalty to my husband. Before I ever cheated on him, men rarely approached me. But now it happens often.

I can read the same thing on men's faces. Whether or not they have a ring, their eyes show their mendacities before they ever utter a sound. Something happens to the thin skin around the eyes when a person's faithless. The skin tenses in such a way that other guileful people understand the tiny movements.

My husband and I are celebrating our tenth anniversary with a party this weekend. If it was anything else, work, friends' party, family event, I'd call off sick. But there's no faking illness for your own anniversary party.

My sister cheated on her husband before they married. I thought it'd stop with their nuptials.

"So did I!" Maricella giggled. "My panic attacks are back." She'd experienced them as a teenager, now they'd returned. "I'm on Xanax," she giggled again, and I thought the medication explained her apparent lack of regret. "But it interferes with the other X."

"Orgasms?"

"Well, that too."

When the shock registered on my face, she added, "Not often. Just once in a while. Women need orgasms!"

That's when I first considered adultery. I felt my listlessness might be due to my lack of orgasms. I'd never cheated on boyfriends, never planned to cheat on my husband. Sometimes, I desire to blame Frank for my infidelity, but I retreat from that. He has problems. He can't sustain an erection. Before we married, we'd successfully engaged in sex a few times accompanied by many loving moments and much attentiveness. He tried Viagra and Levitra, but didn't like the side effects. We created other ways to satisfy our needs. The man was inventive. For a while. A year or so after we'd married, he stopped trying. By all outside views, we're a happily married couple.

I sat him down more than once, said, "I have needs, honey" as gently as possible.

He gave me a half-cocked smile and responded, "I'll talk to my doctor."

He scheduled an appointment. But later, he said, "Oh, damn, I forgot," as if he'd gone to the market for milk, eggs, and bread, and forgot the bread.

When it happened again, I realized he desired a sexless marriage. Maybe he didn't need the physicality or the tenderness. But I did.

A few years ago, he gifted me a sex toy. I became excited by the thought he wanted to try again; I felt heard, validated. But that night, as I inserted the batteries, he asked, "could you do that in the other room?" It was a present to entertain myself.

I needed something more. I want to say I tortured myself before and after the first time I'd strayed. But I didn't. A dinner date proceeded the encounter with lots of talk but, feeling forsaken at home, I went through with it. Afterward, I tiptoed in my guilt, made Sunday breakfast, attempted, once again, to initiate intimacy with Frank. But, alas, that part of our married lives was clearly over. I had a choice: Did I want to stay married? I loved him. Apart from his complete abandonment of my needs, our marriage worked. Everyone thought we were perfect. Sometimes, maybe, that's enough: Good job, good friends, pseudo-loving husband.

My brother, Alex, was unfaithful to his wife once, about five years in. "It's the seven-year itch," he claimed when he secreted me away at Christmas time to confess.

"It hasn't been seven years." I said dryly. That was before I strayed. His seventh anniversary is coming up; I wonder if he'll do it again, use the same excuse. He felt much guiltier than my sister who claimed her culpability, but didn't own it.

Maricella's created stories since she was a child. Alex jokes our baby sister was born lying.

Due on New Year's, she arrived on Christmas. "For the attention," he says.

In some ways, he's right. When she lacked the desired attention, she'd throw a fit. As children, we'd stopped for popcorn at the Target café where she asked for a soda. My mother didn't respond, so Maricella let her body slide to the floor, began flailing her arms, kicking her legs. Alex and I gaped in amazement. My mother's face bled red with large white circles around her eyes and mouth.

Maricella refers to these as panic attacks. "See, I've had them since I was a baby."

I wonder if she's unfaithful because she's not getting enough attention at home; I also wonder if anyone could ever give her enough attention.

In the spring, after my brother's confession, Alex and I stood alone in the yard at a family barbeque. With just us and the smoke rolling over our clothes, I asked, "Why do you think you did it?"

"Will you hush up!" Alex gripped the spatula at his side. "Are you trying to get me busted. It was once!" His guilt manifesting in anger.

"No one's even here," I defended. "They're all in the house."

"Don't ever mention it again, okay?"

I'm friends with his wife. She shares her secrets with me too. At that time in their marriage, they didn't have any problems. "Things are great!" She smiled in a genuine style only honest people maintain.

Even before I fell off the integrity wagon, it never occurred to me to betray my friends' or family's confidences; the importance of curating a safe space to lay one's guilt cannot be compared. Although I preferred not to, I've partaken in their farces; I've pretended to be the friend that kept them out late or, once, imitated my friend's former employer so she could get a new job after being fired. Jamie didn't want her potential employers to know, so when the caller ID on my phone read "JE Corp," I said, "Yes, she was fabulous. We loved her so much, such a hard worker, we were so sorry to see her go," and other things she'd prompted me to say about length of time and money earned. We've all lied about our employment history at one point or another.

The benefit of knowing other people's deceits is becoming adept at reading faces. When most people lie, the skin around their eyes tighten the tiniest bit and the folds around their lips deepen for just a single instant.

Sometimes I test myself. When Jamie claimed she earned sixty thousand dollars, I casually responded, "That's good! I thought they only paid fifty."

Had I been wrong, she would've comfortably chuckled, "no, no," and those lines would loosen. Instead, she shook her head and tightened her smile as she glanced away.

I also assess myself in the mirror. Practicing the explanation that I stayed out shopping longer than I'd expected or I ate dinner with Lilly, I learn to control my tells.

I created her. Lies are easier and my face more relaxed when it's close to the truth. "I'm with Lilly" is closer to a truth because I'm meeting someone he doesn't know, and he doesn't know Lilly. Half-truths are less complicated too because no one gets in trouble. None of my friends need to feign plans should we run into them. It happened once, when someone's husband asked me, "Did you girls enjoy the movie?" An awkward pause ensued before I excused myself. I suppose we all have our own fictions which allows us to live with ourselves.

On Wednesday, I stop at Pete's for a coffee. The line inches along before I finally reach the cashier. "Decaf, please."

"So, you were telling the truth. You don't drink a lot of caffeine." The man too close to me reaches his arm out, hands the cashier a twenty. "I've got this. Make mine a double."

He's a young, attractive man and I've a vague recollection of his face, but I can't place him. As we step away from the cashier to await our drinks, he leans in and whispers, "May I take your order?"

Recognition sparks: the waiter my mother snapped at. I chuckle, "Hello."

"Darren." He shakes my hand as we move to pick up our coffees. "Afternoon off?"

"Lunch." Half-truth. A work errand inspired me to call in a long lunch, and I'm taking my good old time. "You?"

"I live across the street." Darren raises his coffee in the general direction of the high-rise across the road. His eyes linger on my ring finger before returning to meet my gaze. "Great view from my patio and not so crowded." He smiles knowingly. We read each other. There is something about the eyes that is a dead giveaway.

"Nice," I say. He leads the way.

He closes the door behind us and, before I reach the patio door, I feel his hand around my waist as his hot breath wafts down my neck. He takes the coffee cup from my hand, sets it down on a nearby table.

My working lunch gets a little longer.

On Friday, for our tenth anniversary party, my husband wanted a big to-do. I conceded. Guilt. Frank wanted guests, cake, champagne, catering. I called a party planning center and let them take care of it.

I feign getting ready, so he shows the caterers in. He suggests we "make an entrance" after our friends arrive.

"Do you think it's appropriate for us to allow our guests to meander about while we stay up here." I slide the black eye pencil over my lid while seated at my vanity.

"Well, we could give them the impression…" He reaches over from his seat on the bed and caresses my side.

I shoot him a look in the mirror. A sexual innuendo? My face rarely gets away from me. I attempt a mixture of accusatory annoyance with a poker face. I want him to be uncertain so if he calls me on it, I can deny my deep irritation.

He walks away.

Frank answers the door for the first few couples before I descend the stairs. Mine and his families attend along with our friends. The catering company set up in our dining room. I only glance in to make certain they've brought what I asked, but I don't eat and Frank has a glass of champagne waiting for me. I mingle in the living room where most of the guests laugh and chat over the music.

"Honey," Frank whispers. "The candles over the fireplace would look nice lit."

I weave my way through our friends into the kitchen, passing the dining room, to the mud room where the lighters are kept. I reach up to the shelf over the dryer when I hear the door open and click to a close behind me.

I think it's my husband. But an arm slips around me, and then another. I know it's not my Frank, so I turn quickly.

Darren's close cut hair and clean shaven face accompanied by the black and white waiter's uniform make him appear very different, even distinguished.

"Look at you," I whisper.

"When I do these parties, I put on the ritz." His embrace softens. "I'll leave you alone tonight, I just wanted to say hello."

Although rationale dictates I be concerned, my body reacts. I pull him in for a deep kiss. He backs me against the dryer; with his hands on my thighs, he picks me up and sets me on the dryer slowly pushing my dress up.

Sometimes people purposely take risks to unconsciously sabotage situations they are unhappy with. Perhaps I'm a victim of my own unconscious desires just as much as I'm a willing participant in my conscious needs.

Darren slows. "As much as I'd like to, I don't think we should do this here." He kisses me again. "Maybe after the party." Darren lifts me off the dryer gently.

I wipe the lipstick from his mouth; he rubs the smears from mine. I smooth down my dress.

The door opens and, for a single moment, my brother stands backlit before he closes the door. Alex barely met my eyes before retreating. I imagine my face show surprise, not unlike a deer in the headlights. I consider our exact positioning. Was I smoothing my dress, looking at Darren? Was he looking at me, had he backed up enough?

Without another word, I join my husband. Alex mingles, laughs with his wife, smiles if he witnessed nothing. He acts so cool, I wonder if I imagined his figure in the door.

Neither Darren nor I seek one another for the rest of the evening. We don't speak or attempt to make eye contact, not guiltily avoiding it, but these are our separate lives. This is the way real life works.

After the party, Frank strips off his clothes in front of the bathroom door, desirous of getting to the shower quickly. I pick them up, carry them to the laundry basket in our room and toss them on top. One of my blouses lay under the dirty sweats from his regular lunch time work-out. I keep my blouses separate from his exercise gear because I don't want them ruined. When I pull it out, a prescription bottle falls from his pocket. I retrieve it, read the label as I rest on the bottom of the bed.

Cialis. Pleasure washes over me: he talked to his doctor and wanted to surprise me! But a shake of the bottle sounds as if it's not full. I glance at the bottle again. Both the date on the label and the few pills remaining make me rethink.

The shower water ceases, Frank exits with a rush of steam and stands in front of me. His chest is pink from the hot water, the scent of lavender wafts over me. He naturally dark skin appears sensuous against the white cotton.

"You found your surprise." He smiles so genuinely, I almost believe him.

"My surprise?" Maybe I want to be talked out of what I'm thinking.

"Yeah. I went to the doctor. Was going to surprise you." He anticipates my reaction. I think I'm supposed to jump up and hug him, be grateful. But I'm awash in sadness. And, in some small way, I feel relieved of my own guilt.

Tears spontaneously combust from my eyes. I've been such a fool thinking I could read people. Here he was all this time, how much time? lying and having an affair with someone.

"Oh, honey." He sits on the bed and leans in, leaves a soft kiss on my cheek. "I didn't realize you'd be this happy," he says as if he really cares.

How did I miss the signs? How did I miss the puckering of the lines around his eyes, the deepening folds of skin near his mouth that betrays liars for a single instance before they smile?

"It's half full," I choke out.

"What?" He tenderly pulls my hair from my face to look at me.

"It's half full," I declare with much more force than I intend. He's using these little magic pills. But not with me!

"Honey, what are you talking about? What are you saying?" He stands up, steps away. The movements of a liar. Someone trying to cover his tells.

"They're half full." What's my point? Do I want him to confess? Was I going to confess? I want to. I want it all out! I desire honesty, complete and total truth. Then I think better of it. I don't want his admission of guilt. I want it done. I want us, these lies, done.

He takes his towel off, grabs a pair of boxers from the dresser and slips them on. "I don't know what you're thinking. "

I watch him grab a t-shirt, check his face in the mirror. He knows I'm watching. He's buying time too.

Suddenly, I want him to be more wrong than me. I want him out. We've been roommates. We've been each other's safe space when we've had a hard day and needed to vent or needed a hug. We've been each other's assistant, picking up the dry cleaning or taking the car in when the other was busy. That's all we were to each other for the last eight years while he feigned a lack of desire. He'd made me feel unwanted, undesirable, not worth the trouble. I don't need a husband like that. I don't need anyone.

"I guess we should call it done, yeah?" I say as if we burned the soup and didn't care anyway. Frank drops his gaze his hands, before turning to me. "What are you talking about?" He fakes annoyance as if I'd said, let's get a cat knowing he's allergic to cats.

He's good. I think. He's a very good liar. With a half smile at play on my lips, I stand. Did he seriously think I was going to let this go? I stayed in this dry, dead marriage for years while he refused to touch me. It hurt. My smile turns to sadness, but I know that glint of irony surrounds my eyes. I thought I knew the signs of a liar; I'd become filled with my own overconfidence at spotting misdirection, reading an untruth. Perhaps I imagined them all.

Where were the signs of his faithlessness? Every time he said no, or he forgot to talk to the doctor, or he said, "maybe tomorrow," where hid my acute vision to spot the lines moving about his face, the awareness of his hands or his body language? Maybe we let those closest to us lie because we can't believe our loved ones would hurt us. And maybe he knows I've been cheating. Or maybe he hasn't got a clue. Right now, I don't know anything.

I'm looking for those lies around his mouth, the lines of his eyes, the movement of his hand through his hair while he looks at me as if he's dealing with a child who doesn't understand what he's saying.

"You have not touched me in yeeaaarrrsss!" The word drags out as emotion overtakes me. "How long has this been going on?"

"I don't know what you're talking about." Half smile, deep folds around the mouth.

"You're a fucking liar. Do not stand there and treat me like I'm stupid."

He's on me, his face in my face, his arm around me, his hand on the back of my neck. "You don't want me to treat you like you're stupid, then don't act like it." His face contorts in anger, teeth grit, skin around his hair line reddens.

I've never seen this. I'm frightened, and my face shows it. My jaw pulls back in fear, eyes wide, skin whitens. I take deep breaths. Bite my lip. Does he know? But he offers nothing. The anger of a guilty man, caught.

"Be very careful," my calm tone even surprises me. "Your next move will determine whether you go to jail for domestic abuse or if you walk out of here a free man." I control my fear, set my jaw, steel my eyes; or, at least, that's what I try to do. "I suggest you let go of me, pack a bag, and don't let the door hit you in the ass on the way out."

His arms drop as he steps back, stares at me for a moment before moving to the closet for his gym bag, grabs some clothes, and doesn't look back as he walks out the bedroom door. I stand still until I hear the door slam, his car start and pull down the road. Through the window, I see the tail lights brighten as he pauses half way down the street; I wonder if he's considering a return, but then he continues on.

The room is quiet; the air around me cool. I know I'll cry, but not right now. Breath moves freely in and out of my lungs and I feel light. Where the exhaustion of the long day previously dragged on me, I'm no longer tired.

I realize I'm still holding his pills and laugh out loud to myself. That is probably why he paused, I think; he's going to his girlfriend's and doesn't have his pills.

Full of energy, I head downstairs to toss the pills in the trash, lock up the house for the night. The house feels so gloriously big. I find my cell phone and see a message from Darren. It doesn't say Darren, it reads Darlene in case Frank ever saw it. The text's in code: "Lunch soon?" An innocuous message for a secret liaison. But they don't have to be secret anymore. I don't respond to his text; I delete it. There actually doesn't need to be a Darren anymore.

I lock the doors, turn the kitchen nightlight on, and grab a slice of cake from the fridge. Champagne cake, strawberry center, cream frosting with roses. Simply divine, I think as I grab a fork and sit near the kitchen window in the shadows enjoying each and every morsel.

What a relief to not live a lie anymore. I can be me. I can return to the honest person I've always been. No more cheating. No more half-truths. No more attempts to read deception in others or try to hide it on my own dishonest face. It's exhausting. Glorious, glorious freedom.

I leave the plate and fork in the sink and head upstairs to bed, strip naked and cover myself with a sheet. It's a new life.

When my cell rings, I grab it. I assume it's my husband, although I don't know why. I guess I imagine, maybe I hope, he wants to apologize and beg forgiveness, which I will refuse. But it's not him. The caller ID reads Maricella. I answer, assume it's important.

"Leona." The man's deep voice startles me, but I realize it's her husband. "Frank there?"

"What's wrong? Is everything okay?" I ask, worried about my sister.

"No. I need to talk to your husband."

"He's asleep." I refuse to explain the night's events right now. "Is Maricella okay?"

"Yeah." His breath is deep and thick. "He just texted my wife, and I want to know why."

I jump up, hit my head on the headboard. "He what?"

"She says she was with both you and he at lunch today. Is that correct?"

My throat tightens. My mind spins. I try to remember the last time I saw Maricella. Did I hear him right? "She...both of us...lunch...today?" My voice is near whisper; I can barely speak.

"Okay, alright," he says. "As long as you confirm. I'm sorry to have woken you up." The phone clicks to a dead silence.

All the lies I've ever told or heard encircle my head. Our whole lives are built on deceit. I thought I figured everyone out. But I know nothing. I feel lost. Stupid.

I curl around my pillow, sob into it.

Noreen Lace

Air

A crisp breeze bites Rebecca's face. Pain pinches at her as she inhales wakefulness. The sun blinds her and the slight movement of her hand sends her quaking. She tries to make sense of her situation. The stickiness of the sweat soaked polyester seat sucks her in to a reclined position even as the chair pitches. She gasps as she glances around. She's belted in a seat, hanging in a tree.

Although her first instinct is to panic, she also knows she must be calm. She leans toward the thickness of the tree, grasping the dense branch as she moves closer to the trunk and wraps herself around it. The breeze rustles the leaves, nudges at the summer dress and chills her toes through sandals. She heaves her body close to the trunk; the bark scratches her as she moves from one thick branch to the other. Near tears and confused, she slips, pauses, and regains her footing.

When she reaches the bottom, she stands in the sparse grass underneath. Shoulder scraped, leg scratched, hand bruised. The sun hovers high in the sky. The blank empty space around her is broken by sparse trees. Without knowing quite why, she walks east. And, although she's uncertain of many things including her name, she does know which way is east. The trees disappear as dirt and sand turns into a path which leads to the sound of cars. She comes upon a highway and continues along the roadside.

The air thickens, dries, and lies itself flat on the hot black top of the highway. Even though signs indicate a city in the distance, she's overheated and her legs ache. She parks herself on the steal guardrail for a rest and tries to remember how she arrived in a tree in the middle of nowhere; the recollection's there, almost there when a car pauses, distracting her from her thoughts.

Bright pink lipstick and thick, gray hair reveals itself from a lowering tinted window. "Honey, you okay? You need a ride?"

Never get into the car with strangers. But this is an old couple. She's roasting.

"Thank you." She climbs into the back seat.

"How did you come about being out here? Did your car break down?"

"The wind," Rebecca mumbles.

"You look parched." The silken too-tanned, thinning skin of the woman's arm appears over the seat, a bottle of water in hand. "Where you headed?"

She feels sun-blind, fatigued, near passing out; she gulps the water. The car lurches forward and Rebecca slips back on the seat. "Next town is fine." Rebecca nods toward the upcoming town.

The air vent gusts at her mottled hair. Sweat streaks dry in channels on her neck and chest.

The car slows to a stop next to an old phone booth. As they drive off, Rebecca waves like they are the last of her good friends. She picks up the phone and stares at it blankly, listens to the dial tone bleat in her ear. If only she could remember who to call.

Across the street, the wood-planked exterior of the Wickenburg Cafe seems familiar or, at least, comforting. She needs to sit, think. She rushes first to the Ladies' Room where she washes with wet paper towels. Her skin beats red from the spring sun.

"Coffee, hon?" The waitress calls out as Rebecca returns to approach the counter.

"No, thank you." She has nothing. No purse. No bag. No memory of ever having owned these things.

"You here about the job?" The apron passes quickly in front of her.

Rebecca nods, not sure what else to say.

"Is that your family dropped you off?" The waitress tilts her head.

"Yes." Family comes in many definitions, she reasons as she reads the waitress's name from the tag, "Janice."

Janice pulls an application from under the counter. "Ever waitress before?"

"Some years ago." She believes she has served people before. She accepts the offered pen but gets stuck at the very first box: Name. Glancing nervously at the waitress, Rebecca smiles awkwardly. Her mind is space, all dark with little white dots, but none of the dots connect to anything specific.

Jane Doe is too obvious. Smith. Smith and Jones. And Jones. She writes: Ann Jones. Experience: The only restaurant name she remembers is Denny's. She writes that, leaves the rest blank.

"I'll give this to the owner tomorrow. Coffee now?"

"No. Thank you." Rebecca starts to get up.

Janice is older, but strong arms and legs from years of carrying trays, running back and forth. She thinks the young woman seems lost; she sets a cup in front of her. "Free coffee with every application."

A greyhound bus gusts into the gas station across the street. The forty or so people gather together at the corner. Janice reaches for the phone, "Bob. We got a late rush. Some sort of accident out on the highway. I need help!" She slams down the receiver.

"Honey, how about a trial shift?"

Rebecca jumps up. "Yes."

Janice points to the back, "my extra uniform is hanging in the lockers!"

White uniformed, pink aproned, Rebecca grabs menus and leads travelers by twos and threes to open booths or tables, directs the loners to the counter. This vocation seems second nature; she must've served before. However, writing cheques takes longer. She has to refer to the menu. The cook, Henry, gazes over at her once or twice, but decides it could be worse.

When the rush ends and the bus pulls away, Rebecca is thirty-one dollars rich. Moving so fast forced her to forget her aching body. As she settles down to help Janice finish the side work, her feet burn in pain. Sandals are not for waitressing or for walking in the dirt and, especially, not for climbing out of a tree.

"You need a ride home, hon, or your family coming to get you?"

"I don't need a ride," she says as she watches the gas station go dark. It seems the whole town will be dark soon. She wonders where she might spend the night. She changes back into her spring dress, hangs the uniform where she found it and readies herself to face the night. She tells herself, somewhere in town must have a place to sit and put her head down. The day caught up with her; she felt tired enough to drop anywhere.

"What time can you come in tomorrow?" Janice interrupts Rebecca's thoughts

"Anytime."

"Can you do a split?"

"Yes," Rebecca agrees, even though she doesn't know what "split" means.

"Be here at 10:30 to set up, place opens at eleven and you'll work until two. I work two to ten, but then you'll need to return by five to help me with the dinner rush. K?"

"Yes." She understands.

"The morning cook... whatshisname? Pedro will let... Wait." Janice drops her hand in her pocket and fishes out a key. "Now, I'm trusting you with this. Don't lose this or come in here and rob us blind."

Rebecca responds in an exhausted whispery voice. "I would never do that."

Rebecca follows Janice to the parking lot. "You sure you don't need a ride?"

"No, but I better wait out front." She hurries to the street and watches Janice drive off, then she slowly paces in front of the restaurant as if she's waiting for a ride, but Rebecca is considering her choices in the cool, night air. The city becomes dark and quiet, a wind whips up and chills her through. She doesn't want to spend the night in the street. Turning back to the diner, she uses the key, and locks the door behind her. Although her stomach rumbles and her skin is crusted with the day, she collapses in the first booth, curls into a ball, and falls asleep.

In muddled dreams, she's an eagle rising high above the earth and clouds. The strong wind feeds her outstretched wings and the air flutters through her tail feathers. There is no fear as she sails through the sky, circles the ground, and lands confidently in the top of that tree.

The screech of wheels and a bleating horn wakes Rebecca from her slumber. The gas station fills with cars while the city begins to buzz. She stumbles to the kitchen, finds a bag of bread and stuffs one piece after the other into her mouth. When she finishes with the bread, the blueberry pie sitting in the glass cooler makes her mouth water. She grabs a fork and eats it with the whispy cool air soothing her bare feet.

In the employee restroom, she washes as much as she can. For a single moment, an image appears in the mirror, eyes ringed with sadness, smudged make up, but it dissipates with the steam.

Before ten o'clock, she slinks out of the restaurant and walks down the street. There's a pancake house, a few fast food places, and a Waffle's-R-Us all on the same block; in addition to a Wal-greens and supermarket, there are a few local shops. The town is wholly unfamiliar but comforting in its smallness. No where to get lost, she thinks, "or found," a small voice carries on the wind.

By the time she returns, the door is unlocked. "Hello?"

An older man who has a few long strips of hair brushed over his near naked scalp followed by a younger man with a thick bush of black hair and dark eyes appears from the kitchen door.

"I'm the new waitress."

"Do you have a name?" The older man reaches under the counter.

"Yes." She bites her lip. White dots.

"Ann?" he asks.

"Yes." She smiles.

"Bob," he half chuckles and hands her a plastic name tag which reads "Annie."

"This is Peter. He works the day shift with you." Bob turns away, "Janice will give you the rest of the forms later." He pushes through the employees' only kitchen door.

The young man leans close to her. "Pedro. You call me Pedro." His face curls into a scowl before he whips around and disappears through the same door.

Bob stays out of the way, only checking to see how she's doing, but breakfast and lunch are pretty standard with more locals than travelers. Pedro reads her orders, makes the food, and pushes the plates through the serving window without acknowledging her.

When Janice comes in at two p.m., Rebecca strolls to the Walgreens she'd seen earlier. With the money earned, she buys shampoo, soap, a pair of canvas pants and a t-shirt, which reads "Property of Wickenburg Wranglers," even though she doesn't know who or what the Wranglers are.

By four p.m. the sun is too hot to wander aimlessly, and she doesn't have enough money for new shoes; even though her feet hurt, that will have to wait. Her stomach aches for a real meal, so she returns to the café, and asks Janice, "Can I order food and pay later when I make more tips?"

Janice senses there's more to Rebecca's story. "Honey, you can eat free any day you work, half off on the days you don't. K?"

Dropping into a seat at the counter, she notices Pedro watching her through the serving window; she lowers her gaze and contemplates waiting until the night cook comes in.

Pedro bangs through the kitchen door and pours a cup of water; he pauses in front of her. "What do you want? I'll make it good for you."

"Spaghetti," she speaks softly, avoids his harsh eyes. But he doesn't budge. When she dares to raise her gaze, he slides the glass of water across the counter to her.

"It's hot out. Drink a lot of water or you get sick." He pours himself one and returns to the kitchen.

When Pedro returns, he's changed his shirt and, with his softened expression, almost appears a different person. The plate includes meatballs, salad, and garlic bread. She whispers, "thank you," as he leaves for the day.

After work, she waits out front until Janice is out of sight before she slips back to unlock the door. Tonight, she sponge-bathes and washes her hair in the bathroom sink, uses paper towels and the hot air-blower to dry herself.

Relief floods over her. The small room smells of the lavender soap; she closes her eyes, inhales, releasing her breath in long sighs. She's been here before. A warm room, lavender diffusion, purple walls, a thick robe. She teeters and nearly falls over. Her eyes fly open to the eggshell bright of the employee restroom.

She washes the stink from her dress, twists it hard and tight, before hanging it on the back of the door. The new shirt and canvas pants help Rebecca feel like a new person. Yawning, she swings the door open.

A shadowy figure skulks in front of her. Rebecca screams.

"No, no." Pedro backs away, "It's me. It's Pedro. I'm sorry." He raises his hands in mock surrender. "I didn't mean to scare you. I try to tell you I'm here, so not to scare you."

"What are you doing here?"

"Same as you." He tilts his head to the dining room, leads her to the u-shaped booth in the corner where the streetlamps powder them in tawny bisque.

"This is the best place to sit if you're in here alone. No one can see you. If car goes by," he casts a glance to the windows, "the headlights shine in and people can see you. Here, they cannot."

She listens, unmoving.

"That's how I saw you in here last night." He pauses for Rebecca to respond, but she doesn't. "I was mad this morning, but you must not have a place. But you have to share." He presses his finger into the Formica tabletop. "I won't tell. You won't tell. But you have to share."

Rebecca nods. Pedro gets up and goes through the door to the kitchen, and she curls into a ball to sleep.

"What are you doing?" Pedro sets tuna salad sandwiches down; one in front of her, one in front of him. "You don't eat right, you're going to get sick. If you can't work, you can't earn money. If you lose your job, then you can't sleep here. See how it works?"

A car passes, headlights trace the wall, flash reflective ivory showers the all around them, but they stay hidden in the corner umbra.

"Thank you." The two words aren't enough to describe her blooming appreciation.

Pedro takes the plates back to the kitchen, washes them. Before he returns with a pillow, he changes into pajamas.

Rebecca waits until he returns, then begins to curl up.

"Here." He pulls a chair next to the booth. "Lay straight. Put your feet on here." He brings another to the other side. "If you curl up like that, your back will hurt. Then you can't work."

Rebecca stretches out. "Thank you."

He lays his pillow on the other side. In the darkness, they can see each other's outlines in the darkness.

"You have a pillow?"

"Yes." He snaps, but then his tone changes. "Do you need it?" Under the table, he offers the pillow.

"No. Thank you."

"Here, borrow this." He shakes it until she reaches for it.

She bunches it under her head, watches him fold his hands under his head and stare up at the ceiling.

"You can call me Peter if you want," he says.

"What do you prefer?"

"Pedro, but some people don't like to pronounce it."

"Pedro." Her voice is soft. His form fades as her eyes give into sleep. "Why are you so nice to me?" she whispers.

For the first time, he glances over at her; his usual wary countenance softens at the outline of her. "You must be a refugee from something."

Her eyes closed; her breathing shallow.

"Where are you from?" he asks quietly.

"I think I was pretending," her murmur dwindles into sleep.

Pedro watches her breathe the last wakeful inhale. He usually wakes at seven, makes himself breakfast; tomorrow he'll make two. It's not a problem to make another egg, another piece of toast.

They pass weeks doing this, barely speaking during the day, except, once in a while, they cast each other a sentient glance.

One night, Rebecca says, "I saw a room for rent."

"You can't afford it." He seldom turns to her as they lie across from one another.

"You don't even know how much." She believes he's a serious man who rarely smiles.

"You spend too much money. I see you come in here with stuff every day."

"But I need stuff," she defends.

"You need to save money. I can show you. But only if you want."

Rebecca sighs, waits until she sees his expression change. "I thought we could share it," she whispers.

He drums his head from side to side. "No. We are not that way."

"Like this," she says. "Two beds. It has a real shower. We could save money."

"Maybe."

In another few weeks, they share the room with twin size mattresses on the floor and a shower all their own. Their private room is in the back of a small house owned by an elderly couple. They don't ask, but Pedro offers he and Annie are cousins from Guatemala who have all their papers if the family wants to see them. But Rebecca doesn't even have an I.D. to cash her checks. She saves everything in her locker at work, spending her tips when she needs to. When she tells Pedro, he shows her where to go for an I.D. and how to cash her checks, so no one asks questions.

Pedro shows her the second-hand store where, on Wednesdays, everything sells for half price. And he helps her save money; "in case of emergency, you need cash," he says. He saves less than she because he sends money to his family so his sisters can attend school and his mother has enough food to feed the family.

In the mornings, they enter the café separately, five or ten minutes apart, so no one becomes suspicious. However, every night, Pedro returns to walk Rebecca home.

One afternoon, a few months after they find their little room, a family comes in to the cafe. They wear fine white clothes. Two women, sisters maybe, a man, and a young boy who bounces around in his seat and asks for chocolate chip pancakes.

Waffle-House crowd. Rebecca imagines when they leave and start down the street, they'll wish they'd have driven a few more minutes before stopping. She's begun to know the locals and easily recognizes those passing through. She serves the family their French toast-no syrup, tea-no sugar, coffee-no cream, eggs-no oil, toast-no jam and asks if there is anything else before turning away.

The woman pushes herself up in the corner of the booth, "Becky?"

Rebecca curves back as she's done many other times to many other tables. But she's on a beach, her long hair flutters in the wind, the crash of the ocean waves drowns out the sound of everything else. The warm sun teases her senses as she raises her palm to shade her eyes and answers "yeah?" in an exclamation different than one she's ever uttered. That tone is high pitched and hollow.

Suddenly, she's overcome with anxiety. Rebecca pushes out a breath, takes a single step back, and recovers.

"Annie," she taps the name badge with her pen. "Something else?"

The woman doesn't answer; she drops down into the corner of the booth, eyes wide.

Rebecca waits on another table, serves coffee to regulars at the counter without another thought of the woman, the table, the name.

Pedro witnesses the scene through the serving window. Even long after Rebecca stops paying attention to the people at the table, Pedro watches. He doesn't like the way the blonde woman scrutinizes Annie and finds it suspicious that, the moment the family leaves, the woman pulls out her cell phone and keeps glancing back at the café.

The next day a man comes in and sits at the counter. He's not local and doesn't seem to be in a hurry to get on with his travels.

"Coffee?" Rebecca barely notices him.

"Yes." His voice muffled.

"Cream, sugar?"

He stares at Rebecca's face, takes a moment to glance around the café to see who might notice. No one does, including Rebecca.

She hands him a menu. "Lunch or just pie?"

"Pie."

"We got peach, apple, and chocolate silk." The chocolate's leftover from yesterday; she needs to upsell that one. "Chocolate silk is very good."

"Apple." The word lumps in his throat. "My wife used to make apple pie." The sentence floats slowly from his lips as if he's trying to hang on to the sound of it. The consonants are thick and round, the vowels thin like broth, Rebecca winds around. He's familiar, as if from a movie. She remembers the scene. The actor stands tall and straight, the lady rises on to the tips of her toes. She wants to reach that kiss, trying hard to please, to reach the tiny, somehow resistant, puckered-offering from his lips.

Rebecca's stomach twists raw.

"Ice cream?" She twirls away.

His shoulders drop. He focuses on Rebecca, inspects her every move. She serves him the pie without looking at him, waits on other customers, cleans the counter. When she slides the cheque across the counter, he stands and tries to grab her wrist.

Pedro appears with a steel spatula between him and the stranger, Rebecca tucked safely behind him.

"You do not put your hands on people here."

"She looks like someone." The man flexes his jaw. "Rebecca? Is it you? What happened to you?" He leans his tall body further over the counter.

Pedro places his arm protectively in front of Rebecca. "This is Annie. You can't read? You go now."

Some of the regulars, a trucker, a guy from the shoe store down the street, another neighbor, stand ready.

The stranger backs away. "She was lost." The man runs his hand through his streaked-blonde hair, steps back. "I'll go."

After he's gone, Pedro waves his hand to tell the customers everything is okay. He touches his hand to Rebecca's shoulder. "Are you okay?"

Rebecca nods, sucks in small puffs of air through her nostrils.

"Take a deep breath." Pedro waits. "Do you know that man?"

She shimmies her head. "I think he was in a movie."

Pedro pats her shoulder. "I will not let anyone happen to you." He hears his mistake but doesn't correct himself.

The incident blanches in a day or so, just as a young couple arrive at the cafe. Their nuanced style, clean cut appearance, and apprehensive glances at one another say they are not locals.

"We're from Malibu." The woman seems to inspect Rebecca

"What can I get for you?" The couple receive the same warm smile travelers from Detroit or Timbuktu do.

"I'm Misty." Her tone speaks of one-time cheerleader confidence.

"Pretty name." Rebecca turns to the young man who stares at the Formica topped table.

"Sean," he says flatly. He's tall and thin, a pale string bean with a protruding Adam's apple.

"Cokes?"

The couple arch their brows. "We never drink soda," Misty pauses but, when she doesn't get a response, she announces, "Iced tea."

"Lemonade," Sean's pointed apple bobs.

They lean in and share hushed half syllables until Rebecca sets the cold-sweating glasses on paper coasters in front of them. "You look familiar," the girl says. "Are you from California?"

Rebecca's mind can't form a single picture of California, but a movie reel plays in her head, beaches, palm trees, girls bouncing in red bathing suits. "Where you're from doesn't matter; it's where you are," she sighs softly, not certain she even said it aloud.

"She's from Guatemala. Like me. We came together," Pedro calls through the serving window.

They all turn toward the voice, then back to one another. Rebecca snickers, amused. "Burgers?"

They say they need more time, so Rebecca walks away.

The young woman stalks out, tea untouched, a slight sneer in Rebecca's direction. The young man lays a twenty on the counter where Rebecca stands; his face is unemotional, flat lines and unmoving features. Rebecca steps to the door to watch them go.

There's more to that movie. Not the girls in bathing suits movie. Another one.

Rebecca searches those white dots in the dark spaces that have filled with customers and orders and tips and new names and places. If she tries hard enough, maybe she can connect them. But her stomach twists and her eyes wince.

"Are you okay?" Pedro calls through the order window.

As they walk home in the summer heat, Pedro murmurs to her, "Is there something you're keeping from me?"

"No. I would not."

"Did you know those people who came today?"

"Which ones?"

"That couple."

"I don't know them."

"I think they know you." They continue in silence. He heard Janice tell Bob the girl had a car accident. Although Pedro didn't notice a bump on Rebecca's head, he remembers the scratches on her arms and legs.

"People always think they know you," she whispers. "Peter. Pedro." The names slide out in the night between them.

The next day as Rebecca returns for her five o'clock shift, Pedro eats at the table reserved for the staff. She tosses him that sideways glance and a slight smile that might betray their secret friendship if anyone bothered to notice. Pedro wears a grim expression most of the time, but she's grown used to his softened gaze when they share that knowing flash in the bright light of the diner or as they whisper in hushed tones in the shadows of their little room before they fall asleep. Sometimes, she makes him laugh. She appreciates the crack of a slow smile across his face or his rare and uncontrollable belly busting chortle.

Bob slips in the front door behind her. He rarely returns in the evenings, so Pedro takes notice. Bob touches Rebecca's shoulder, something he's not done before, and leans in to her, "This man says he's gotta talk to you." He motions to a heavy, freckled man in an expensive brown suit sipping coffee at the counter.

Rebecca approaches him without hesitation. "What can I help you with?"

The man raises his gaze, takes in the whole of her, which makes her step back. Bob touches her again and waves them toward the corner booth. This is where they hold meetings, where Bob does his paperwork, where the employees eat, like Pedro does now.

"Peter, beat it." Bob thumbs him away. Pedro moves his meal to the counter.

The man is older; he pushes his body in the booth across from Rebecca. He gulps in big breaths of air as he slides his leather briefcase onto the table top, opens it between him and her. He sorts through papers and removes a manila folder.

"Mrs. Harper, I'm Jeff Ross, your husband's attorney."

"Annie Jones," she clears her throat, starts to slide out of the booth.

Bob holds his hand out, "Just listen to him."

She turns from Bob to the big man. His breath is an effort, his movements are an effort, and although she doesn't judge the people she serves, he doesn't seem particularly nice.

"Of course. Mrs. Jones."

"Miss." Rebecca's hands shake. She watches Bob disappear through the employees' only door, then meets Pedro's eyes. He's close if she needs him.

"It seems, Miss Jones, you may well be this missing woman from California, Rebecca Harper, presumed lost in a plane crash April 28th of this year." As he continues to speak, he pushes pictures across the table. There's a woman who looks like Rebecca. A photograph of the doppelganger with the man who tried to grab her wrist, and another of them with the younger couple who came in the other day. The men could be brothers. And although the women are both blonde haired and light eyed, they are not sisters. Rebecca senses, they are not friends either. Although their mouths are upturned in a smile, their eyes don't shine. They stand barefooted in the sand, a big house behind them. The wind rustling their hair and clothes. The others have their arms around one another; her likeness clasps her hands in front, leans away from them. The house behind them feels empty; it's devoid of something. But what?

The answer's somewhere, on the breeze that blew back their hair, in those white points of lights that she barely considers anymore.

She studies the could-be-actor who grabbed at her; the film rolls, her on tippy toes reaching for that kiss, but she can't complete the scene. There are rough hands on her shoulders. The heroine thins to flatness, begins to fade and the movie ends, blacked out by raised voices, angry words.

Rebecca becomes nauseous. She pushes the photographs back to the attorney and puffs in deep breaths.

The movie ended badly.

Rebecca's voice shakes. "That's not... it's mean." The words jumble in her mouth and nothing else comes out. The woman does not look like her. Rebecca's hair is not blonde. Her dark roots prove that. Her skin is not light. She is sun-browned and likes it. Her name is not Rebecca or Becky or even Becks. She's not sure what it is, but Ann sounds better, especially the way Pedro calls her Annie when they go to sleep at night, as if the middle of her name gets stuck on his tongue and he has to push it the rest of the way out, Awn-knee. The way it slips off Janice's tongue, simple and sleek, A-nee, or the way Bob barks it out, Ann. That's her name. And this is who she is.

Pedro sets a glass of water in front of her. "Drink this," he says more softly than he's ever spoken to her.

Bob calls Pedro in the back with a single finger. "What are you doing?"

"I don't want that man hurting Annie."

"They've got business. You get on home now."

Pedro waits across the street in a patch of grass shaded by a large tree. They won't bother to see him here, but he can watch, make sure no one tries to take Annie if she doesn't want to go.

Jeff Ross nods, his jowls shimmy, "It seems there was a loss of cabin pressure when the plane dropped. The lack of oxygen can cause a loss of consciousness and, if deprived of air long enough, can cause memory loss, which may or may not be temporary. We can get you the very best medical care, Mrs. Harper. Anything you need."

Rebecca shakes her head, back and forth in tiny little movements like a bobble head broken on its own axis. She stands, bites her whole mouth closed, and moves away from the booth. "You have to go. This is my shift."

Bob appears from behind the door. "You heard Miss Jones. Get on out now."

The attorney struggles from the booth, gathers his papers, lumbers out.

That night, Rebecca starts to walk down the street before Janice drives off, before Pedro jogs over. They walk without talking, as if they are both tired even though they're not.

"What if it's true?" Padro interrupts the silence.

She keeps her gaze on the cracks in the sidewalk. "The only thing I know to be true is right here in front of me now."

They remain quiet for a while longer. He puts his arm around her for the very first time.

"The rest is like a movie that won't play," she says as they approach the house with their little room in the back. "I don't think it was a good movie either."

The next day, Pedro and Rebecca come in together, unconcerned what Bob or anyone else might figure out. The door opens, closes. Rebecca starts to say hello, but it's the man who reached over the counter for her, the man from the pictures, the image from the movie clip in her head.

She stands motionless.

"Honey," he steps closer to her. "You can't tell me you want this life over ours – in Malibu – on the beach – where you never have to lift a finger."

His words feel empty. Maybe it's that house. Or maybe it's who she was. None of it means anything at all to who she is.

Pedro slams the door open and stands beside Rebecca. He reaches his arm gently around her waist.

The man ignores Pedro's presence. "Do you have any idea what people are saying?" His voice turns to a growl and Rebecca's insides grate. "You are Rebecca Harper. I am your husband!"

"This is Annie Jones Garcia. I am her husband," Pedro states.

Rebecca turns from Mr. Harper to Pedro. She wants to laugh.

Mr. Harper snaps his arm across the counter, tries to snatch Rebecca's wrist in his grasp, but Pedro captures Mr. Harper's instead.

"Stop!" Somehow, she feels stronger than she thinks she ever has. No one will make her do what she doesn't want to do, not ever again.

"Pedro, give me one minute please." Rebecca curls around the cash machine and leads Mr. Harper outside.

"What the hell is wrong with you, Rebecca?" The man towers over her.

Rebecca's response is firm, and too quiet for Pedro to hear.

"You need to get your ass home and back to your role in our household."

Her head buzzes as a thick anger wells from a hurt place she no longer owns. She shakes it off, calms herself.

"Mr. Harper," Rebecca's voice raises, not in anger, but in confidence. "This is my home. And this is who I am."

"Your true life is with me at our home." His face flushes with frustration, his hands curl into fists. Pedro moves closer to the door to be seen, to act if needed.

Rebecca thinks of the stories the customers tell of what they want and what they have and who they wish they were. None of it is real. It all changes with the breeze. Only moments are true. "The only true life is the one we are living at this moment."

Mr. Harper turns, his lip curls to a snarl, and he stalks away.

Rebecca returns to the cash register. She can feel Pedro watching her. "You want to be my husband?" She wants him to laugh.

Pedro angles his body toward the door of the kitchen, "I cannot marry you. I have a wife."

"In Guatemala?" Rebecca smirks.

He rounds back to her. "I can take you away," he says. "If that man will give you problems, I can take you home to my mother's house. You will be safe there." His urgent breath wafts across her cheeks.

She wants to hug him; she's never had a better friend than he is right now. She touches his hands instead. "We can breathe only one breath at a time, just as we can only live one life at a time. My life is here and now. I won't run or hide from anything."

Without another word, he returns to his work in the kitchen. Rebecca wonders if the wind will change direction tonight as Pedro walks her home in the cool evening air. There's no reason to rush it, no reason to wish for it. The air changes direction, it always does, and it takes you places, leaves you other places. All you have to do is let it carry you.

Many thanks to my students for being cover models!

ACKNOWLEDGEMENTS:

- The Healer's Daughter appeared in The Ear's May 2019 Issue

- How to Throw a Psychic a Surprise Party appeared in The Oleander Review March 2018

- Friends, Lovers, and Liars appeared in Home Renovation by Pilcrow and Dagger in April 2019

- Bowie and The Basket Case appeared in ID Press's Crime edition – 2019

ABOUT THE AUTHOR

Noreen Lace has published fiction, memoir, and poetry in The Chicago Tribune's Printers Row Journal, The Maine Review, and The Oleander Review, among others. "Memorial Day Death Watch," a memoir of her father's passing, placed as a finalist in Writer Advice while her poem, "All at Once," was a finalist in Medusa's Laugh. *Eddy*, a fictional account of Edgar Allan Poe's overdose in 1848, was released January 2018. www.NoreenLace.com

Also by Noreen Lace:

Eddy – January 2018

West End – Oct 2016

~

Also by REaDLips Press:

The Lone Escapist by Dan Rhys

I, Polyphemus by Ron Terranova

The Last Night in Granada by Chris Pellezzari